HOME
THROUGH
THE DARK

HOME
THROUGH
THE DARK
a novel of suspense

A NTHEA
FRASER

Dodd, Mead & Company, New York

First published in the United States 1976

Printed in the United States of America
by The Haddon Craftsmen, Inc., Scranton, Penna.

Library of Congress Cataloging in Publication Data

Fraser, Anthea.
    Home through the dark.

    I. Title.
PZ4.F8413Ho4 [PR6056.R286] 823'.9'14 76-6873
ISBN 0-396-07286-0

". . .when the stage lights are down and the doors open and it's time to go home through the dark."

From *The Observer's* obituary of Maurice Chevalier,
January 1972

HOME
THROUGH
THE DARK

Chapter 1

THE Fiat was on top of me before I'd even registered its approach. One moment the long country road stretched behind me, empty except for the little Morris I'd overtaken a few minutes previously; the next, with a terrifying screech of tires, the Fiat was alongside, scraping along the body of my own car with a scream of tortured metal and spinning me judderingly off the road. I was too busy fighting to remain upright to have time to register its number. In any case, it was out of sight almost immediately. I switched off the engine and rested my forehead on the steering wheel, waiting for the sick pounding of my heart to subside. All in all, this had not been my day.

There was the slam of a car door, the sound of hurrying footsteps, and a breathless voice above me enquired, "Are you all right?"

I raised my head to see the woman from the Morris regarding me anxiously, and gave her a shaky smile. "Incredibly enough, yes, thanks!"

"I suppose you hadn't time to get his number?"

"No."

"Blasted maniac! There's a nasty scratch along the side here. You're quite sure you're not hurt?"

"Quite, really. It was a lucky escape though. If there'd been a tree in the way—"

"I know. Even so, you look pretty badly shaken. Have you far to go?"

I hesitated. I could hardly say I had no idea where I was going, that I'd only turned off the coast road because it was jammed with traffic and anyway one place was much the same as another in my present mood. "How far's the nearest town?"

"Westhampton's only a couple of miles along the road."

Westhampton. I'd heard the name recently in some connection. "I should think that would do," I said without interest.

"You mean you've nowhere definitely in mind?"

"Not really. I was intending to book in at a hotel wherever I happened to be."

"I might be able to help, then. I work at the George, right in the heart of the town. I'm sure you'd be comfortable there. Of course," she added awkwardly, "if you'd rather look round for something smaller—"

"No, no, I'm sure the George would do admirably."

"Then I suggest we lock up your car and leave it here for one of the garage attendants to collect. I really don't think you're up to driving at the moment."

"Thank you," I said gratefully; "that would be a relief."

Between us we pulled up the hood, extracted the suitcases

I'd packed so haphazardly a few hours previously, and walked back to the parked Morris. My legs felt like cotton wool and I realized I was still shaking.

"My name's Baillie, by the way—Margaret Baillie."

"Virginia Durrell," I said, astonishing myself. It was as easy as that, an almost instinctive wiping of the slate.

"I gather you've never been to Westhampton before?" she went on. "I'm sure you'll like it—it's a very restful kind of town. Are you on holiday?"

I said carefully, "I suppose you could call it that. A rather extended one, though."

She glanced at me curiously but I didn't elaborate and she didn't press the point. We had come into the outskirts of the town by this time and I looked with the first flicker of interest at the dignified old houses in their large gardens, the quiet parks and tree-lined roads. After sweltering in London during the hottest September for thirty years, it struck me that I could do a lot worse than stay here while I sorted out my long-term plans.

Westhampton seemed to have made few concessions to the twentieth century. Its shops were for the most part bow-fronted and diamond-paned like the illustration on a box of Quality Street. It was only at the lower end of the High Street that I noticed almost with a sense of shock a few of the better-known multiples.

"The Avenue has the best shops," Mrs. Baillie was saying, expertly bypassing a crocodile of uniformed schoolgirls. "It's built on the same lines as Southport and Cheltenham—you know, gardens and offices one side and shops the other. Here's the George now. I'll take you in first and then if you

3

give me the keys, Jack can go straight back and collect your car."

In the moment that she took to come round to my side and open the door, I slipped off my wedding ring and dropped it into my bag. If Westhampton was to be my home for the next few weeks—and from what I'd seen of it I doubted if I should find anywhere better—then I wanted no awkward questions about an absent husband. I had introduced myself almost without thinking as Virginia Durrell and Virginia Durrell I should remain. Miss.

I was glad of Mrs. Baillie's arm as she helped me up the stone steps. It had been a day of shocks, and reaction was beginning to set in.

"Jane—" The girl at the reception desk looked up. "Is Number Seventeen still empty? Good. Give me the key, will you? The registering can wait for the moment. This lady's just had a slight accident in her car and she's still rather shaken." She took my arm again. "The lifts are over here, Mrs. Durrell."

"It's 'Miss,' actually," I murmured with difficulty.

"I beg your pardon?"

I felt an unwelcome colour heat my face. *"Miss* Durrell," I repeated with a hint of defiance.

Her eyes went quickly to my hand, then to my face. "I'm so sorry," she said quietly. She knew, of course, that I was lying: the first thing one woman notices about another, Women's Lib or no, is whether she is wearing a ring. However, it was none of her business and she had acknowledged the fact. To my relief the lift arrived and we went up to the first floor and she showed me into a pleasant room at the side of the hotel overlooking its gardens.

4

"You might like to rest up here for a while. That chair's very comfortable. Shall I order you some afternoon tea?"

"Thank you, that would be very welcome. And, Mrs. Baillie, I really am grateful for all you've done." And for not giving me away downstairs. She smiled.

"Not at all. I'm sure a rest and perhaps a leisurely bath will put you right now. Don't worry about the car. I'll see to it. Dinner is from six-thirty, by the way." The door closed behind her. I was alone. More alone than I'd ever been.

Slowly I moved across the room and stood leaning on the windowsill staring unseeingly down at the riot of colours in the flower beds below. Somewhere near at hand a clock struck five. This time yesterday I had been happily removing dead roses from the cut-glass bowl, one ear open for Carl's key in the door.

The enormity of my loss welled up and threatened to swamp me. What a blind, trusting fool I'd been! The flower beds spun crazily in a prism of tears. Shakily I lowered myself into the easy chair and stared bleakly round the pleasant room. I hadn't thought to ask how much it would be, but obviously I shouldn't be able to stay here long. Thank heaven I'd at least had the sense to stop at the bank and cash a check. No doubt there was a local branch who would arrange credit facilities, but even so, with the future suddenly so uncertain, I couldn't afford extravagances.

A knock on the door interrupted my thoughts and heralded tea. The smiling girl brought over a low table to where I sat and laid down the tray appetizingly set with scones, bread and butter and a selection of fancy cakes. As I started to eat, I realized that at least part of the emptiness inside me was due to the fact that I'd had nothing since breakfast. The

5

reason for my disastrously unexpected call at the theatre had been to persuade Carl to take me out to lunch.

Oh, God! My teeth rattled against the cup and I set it down quickly. Ironically, it was only last week that I'd heard him complaining to Fred that the lock on his office door was out of alignment and didn't always click into place. After that frozen moment in the doorway I had turned and fled, my only coherent thought being to put the greatest possible distance between us with the greatest possible speed.

Back at the elegant, impervious flat I had flung things at random into the two cases, dashed out to the car again and begun my flight in earnest. I did in fact pause for one moment to wonder where the passport was before remembering that, in this most unfair of worlds, I couldn't use it without Carl anyway, which effectively ruled out the Continent as a bolt hole. I suppose subconsciously I had felt that the south coast was the next best thing. Not that it mattered. Nothing mattered any more.

I pushed the table away and stood up quickly. Leonie Pratt, of all people! How ludicrous they'd looked, their faces, stupid with surprise, turned towards me. By now Carl would doubtless be ringing round our friends trying to find out where I was. Well, let him. I had no intention of contacting him. I wanted nothing more from him. In fact, I told myself shakily, I wanted nothing from anybody. I had no family and our friends were essentially Carl's anyway. It was my own fault for marrying someone so completely alien to my own background.

Slowly I turned from the window and looked with disinterest at the cases containing my belongings. Heaven knew what I'd put in them. It would be sheer luck if I found such essentials as a toothbrush and nightdress. Luck, however, was with me that far. I hung up a few dresses in the vast reaches of the wardrobe, laid out my makeup case and hairbrush on the austere dressing table and told myself firmly that as this was the only home I had for the moment, I'd better make the most of it. No fragrant rosebuds in cut-glass bowls here. And at that recurring memory the tears finally came, flooding over me with all the force of a tidal wave and dragging me down in their fierce undertow until I was lost in a total abandonment of grief.

I had always known, of course, that Carl was irresistible to women; his fame, his striking good looks and his quite genuine charm attracted them in equal measure. I had also acknowledged, painfully, that it was beyond his power, perhaps even his inclination, to withstand their blandishments. There was a deep, basic need in him, as in most actors, for admiration and acclaim, a continual compulsion to prove to himself and everyone else that he wasn't losing his talent or his popularity. It had been hard for me to accept at first that Carl of all people, so arrogant, so blatantly in command of every situation, should suffer this basic insecurity.

"But, darling!" I'd expostulated. "You're right at the top of the tree!" He had smiled ruefully. "And, my love, when one is at the top, the only direction one can go is down!"

So I had tried hard not to resent the endless flirtations and easy kisses which made up so large a portion of our social life. In the world of the theatre, I was given to understand, these things were a matter of course and no one but a rather stuffy schoolmistress could possibly take objection to them.

7

But even these apparently had not been enough.

A swift mental review of the last few months presented me with a list of at least six women who undoubtedly had the time and inclination, and quite possibly the opportunity, for an affair with Carl. It had simply never occurred to me that he would betray me that far. Obviously I'd been mistaken. A platonic friendship with my husband was seemingly impossible for any woman. Even Madame Lefevre flirted with him outrageously, and she was well over sixty. Or at least she had done, until news of her son's death had completely demoralized her, poor soul.

I sat up at last, tentatively fingering my swollen eyelids. If I were to be presentable for dinner in the hotel dining room, it was time to see about repairing the ravages of my tears.

When, an hour later, I ventured downstairs, it was to find the garage attendant waiting for me in the hall. "Miss Durrell?" He handed me the car keys. "Well, we've got her safely back, miss, and she doesn't seem in bad shape. Just that nasty scrape along the offside door. Do you want us to touch it up for you, or will it be an insurance job?"

I smiled slightly, thinking of Carl's precious No Claim bonus. "There's not much point in bothering, if you can do it. After all, I don't know who the culprit was. I'll just have to write the whole thing off to experience."

"But you'll put the police onto him, surely? They could trace him. He's bound to have a dirty great mark along his own door."

But I didn't want the police's notice any more than my unknown assailant would. "It's not worth it, honestly. No real harm was done."

8

"Not this time maybe," returned my champion darkly, "but he shouldn't be allowed to get away with it. Mrs. Baillie said he didn't even stop to see if you was hurt, and he must have seen you spinning, in his rear-view mirror. Didn't you get a look at him at all?"

"Only an impression of dark hair and sunglasses. Not much help. Really, I'd rather forget the whole thing. Just do what you can to repair the damage, will you? And thank you for bringing her back." I fumbled in my purse and handed him a pound note, which he made a play of not wanting to take, and by the time his scruples had been honourably set aside and he went on his way, people were beginning to make their way through to the dining room.

I was relieved to be directed to a small table over by the window, from where I could study my fellow diners in relative privacy. The George was obviously principally a businessman's hotel, with only a sprinkling of elderly residents. After an initial glance no one paid me any attention and the slight puffiness round my eyes remained blessedly undetected.

It was eight-fifteen when I finished my meal and the evening stretched emptily ahead of me as, I realized with rising panic, would every other evening from now on. Already it was almost dark outside and my initial idea of a walk through the town was not feasible. I glanced into the large, impersonal lounge just off the hall, and immediately rejected its station waiting-room atmosphere. There was a stand of paperbacks by the reception desk and I was turning it idly when the girl called me across.

"Miss Durrell, I wonder if you'd mind registering now?"

9

It was only when I had signed my name that I realized I could hardly fill in the address of the Chelsea flat. "I'm just in the process of moving," I said quickly. "What shall I put, 'No fixed address'?"

The girl smiled. "That might alarm the other guests! Never mind, just leave that column blank for now. Can you give me any idea of how long you'll be staying?"

"Not at the moment. I shall be going to an estate agent tomorrow to see if they have any furnished flats available. If I can find somewhere suitable, I'll move in right away." I held up the paperback I had selected to help me pass the evening. "Can I pay you for this? And is there a Residents' Lounge anywhere?"

"Yes—down that passage on your right—it's marked on the door."

The Residents' Lounge, though smaller, looked no more inviting than the other and I was subjected to slightly disapproving stares from the assorted occupants. A police serial was in full spate on the television. I sat down as inconspicuously as possible and opened my book, but the initial concentration required to awaken interest in it was beyond me. My mind circled repeatedly round Carl and Leonie and belatedly I began to wonder if I had done the right thing in running away. I must certainly have branded myself forever as the stuffy schoolmistress he had probably always suspected. Might it not have been more dignified to have returned to the flat and left to Carl the onus of coming back to face me? But I knew I could not have remained calm and dignified and the whole thing would have degenerated into bitter accusations. Under such circumstances things might have been said which would have endangered our future together just as surely as I had done by leaving without waiting to hear his excuses. After all, what excuses could he possibly have?

The police serial finished and the news came on. More bombs in London—a sudden, aching anxiety for Carl which I quickly crushed. But might not a theatre appear to some warped mind as an ideal place for an explosion? I clenched my teeth and fixed my attention on the announcer. The news tailed off into the weather forecast. The hot weather was expected to continue.

I had picked up my book again when the next words from the television electrified me. "And now on our midweek discussion program we are screening a live interview with Carl Clements."

For the second time that day my first instinct was flight, but quite suddenly I hadn't even the strength to get to my feet. And already Carl's face was on the screen, so familiar in every contour that I couldn't tear myself away, couldn't believe that the tie between us had been so abruptly broken. I remembered now that he had mentioned the program— could it really have been only this morning, at breakfast? "Come to the theatre with me, Gin, and we'll go on for supper afterwards." He hated live television, complaining that he always felt under-rehearsed, and I'd been glad that he wanted my support in the studio audience.

Certainly he was not his usual suave self this evening. Twice the interviewer had to repeat a question, once Carl's reply was completely off the mark, and once, at a relatively innocuous question, he very nearly lost his temper. No doubt, I thought with savage satisfaction, he was wondering

11

where I was, whether I would be back at the flat by the time he got home.

"It seems some time since we've seen you on the stage yourself, Mr. Clements, though I know, of course, that you're producing the play at the Playhouse. Are you intending to do less acting in the future and concentrate on producing?"

Carl shifted on his chair, glanced openly at his watch. "Not at all, no. In fact I shall be appearing in a new production of *Richard the Third* early in December."

I stopped listening to the exchange, concentrating on Carl's obvious unease. Should I perhaps ring him at the flat later, if only to let him know that I hadn't thrown myself in the river? But there was nothing else to say. By running away I had effectively burned my boats. I had forestalled any attempt of his to put things right and my pride would not now let me make the first move towards reconciliation.

A sudden rush of helpless tears blurred his image and by the time I had collected myself again the interviewer was smoothly bringing the program to a close. At last this horrible, traumatic day was almost over. With the unread paperback clasped like a talisman, I left the room and went swiftly up to bed.

Chapter 2

THE next morning, waking in an unfamiliar room and the rushing back of full consciousness brought a renewed wave of desolation, only slightly mitigated by the sunshine that was flooding into the room. Carl would still be asleep, his hair over his face and one arm flung across my empty side of the bed.

I swung my legs over the side of the bed, determining to clamp down on all thoughts of Carl until I had more control of myself. In any case, I told myself severely, turning the bath taps on full, my position was by no means unique and I was better placed than most. There could be few women who had both the financial independence and the complete lack of ties which had made my own immediate withdrawal feasible. There were, incredibly, a few blessings still left to be counted and not the least was that this was a new day and I could do something positive about finding somewhere to live.

Westhampton when I ventured out a couple of hours later lightened my self-pity still further. It was a gracious, well-proportioned town of clean buildings and a leisurely, unhurried atmosphere. I made my way down the narrow High Street, peering into the windows of antique shops and little grocers still old-fashionedly redolent of roasting coffee, and eventually turned the corner which brought me out halfway down the elegant Avenue.

On the opposite side from where I stood, grass and flower beds offered a pleasant walk and the opportunity to sit beside sparkling fountains, while the colonnaded row of buildings behind them consisted apparently of banks, solicitors' offices, and, I hoped, estate agents'.

I crossed the wide road, threaded my way round a fountain, and almost immediately came upon what I was looking for. The legend on the glass read "Culpepper, Simpson and Clark, Auctioneers and Estate Agents." I pushed open the door and went in. The outer office was deserted and the two glass doors in the handsome walnut partition at the back remained firmly closed. There was a bell on the counter and I rang it, idly running my eye down the lists of properties displayed.

Nobody came. Outside the windows the fountains played and across the road I could see the moving, brightly coloured throng of morning shoppers.

I rang the bell again, with less hope, and it was echoed almost immediately by the sudden shrilling of the telephone on the counter beside me. Surely the joint summons would bring someone running? It takes a lot of will power to let a telephone ring unanswered, even when it is not your own, and the aftermath of yesterday's distress had left me with a tendency to a headache. I picked up the receiver therefore, intending to say that the office appeared to be deserted, but

14

before I could speak a low voice broke in with an undercurrent of urgency: "Are you alone?"

Off balance, I stammered, "Er—yes, I—"

"Then shut up and listen. I've not much time. It went like a dream— he never knew what hit him! Now all we need is the lolly. Bring the note as soon as you can in a plain envelope—Picardy 127. But for God's sake don't knock or anything till you hear the tune and know the coast's clear. Okay? See you."

The phone clicked in my ear. I stood blankly holding it while the incredible phrases repeated themselves senselessly in my head. After a moment I carefully replaced the receiver and ran my hands down my skirt. Outside, a passing car hooted suddenly and my heart leaped to my throat. My original intention of leaving a message for the absent staff was hardly applicable now. In fact, if anyone learned what I had inadvertently overheard—

Before the thought had fully formulated, I was outside in the sunshine, walking quickly up the road. A swift glance over my shoulder showed the path clear behind me. As far as I could tell, no one had seen me emerge. The lolly—note in a plain envelope—wait till you hear the tune. Shades of Harry Lime, I thought, but the parallel wasn't as amusing as I'd supposed.

I was still walking swiftly up the road. What would the caller do when he realized the wrong person had received his message? What *could* he do? There was nothing whatsoever to link me with it. If I'd spoken at all, it had been no more than a word, and who in this town could recognize my voice from that?

"Never knew what hit him." Was that a colloquialism or

had it been meant literally? I shivered in the warm sunshine. Looking about me at this lovely town and its inhabitants going peacefully about their everyday business, the whole thing seemed ludicrous. But no more ludicrous than bombs in Oxford Street. Heaven help us, we were beginning to accept the macabre, the distorted, almost without questioning it.

My swift progress had brought me to the end of the parade and as luck would have it, the last doorway happened to be that of another estate agent. This time I glanced cautiously inside and was reassured to see a girl sitting at a desk typing. I pushed open the door and went in.

I imagine something of my agitation must have communicated itself to the man sitting opposite me across the wide expanse of desk, and not unnaturally he put it down to acute anxiety to find somewhere to live. His manner became positively avuncular.

"Now don't worry, Miss Durrell, I'm sure we'll find somewhere to suit you, though the amount of rent you have in mind is rather limiting. However, we'll do our best."

Two hours later, my agitation had increased rather than otherwise. A succession of dreary, boxlike flats was behind us, each one a mockery of the gracious Chelsea apartment that had so recently been home. Although I had not anticipated finding anything in that class, it was impossible to imagine myself living in any of these.

Back in the car again, Mr. Henry said tentatively, "Miss Durrell, there's no chance of your raising the figure at all? I have in mind one particular property which I'm sure would appeal to you. It only came on the market last weekend; the owner has been sent abroad on business and wants to let it for six months. I'm sure it's very much what you're looking for, but I'm afraid it's also considerably more expensive."

"Well, on the strength of what we've seen so far, I'll obviously have to raise my sites a little."

"Let me at least show you the Beeches and then we can discuss the financial implications more fully."

Financial implications—the words had a rather forbidding ring. Thank goodness for the small legacies from my parents which careful investment had substantially increased over the years. At least I shouldn't be in the undignified position of having to appeal to Carl for help.

We were now leaving the depressing streets of shabby-genteel houses and moving into a much more pleasant district with wide, tree-lined roads like those I had seen yesterday with Mrs. Baillie.

"Almost there," Mr. Henry said rallyingly, and we turned into a handsome square, the centre of which was entirely filled with a park. "It's over on our right now, but since it's 'one way,' we have to go round three sides of the square to get there. A lovely position, I'm sure you'll agree."

I was straining to look back over my shoulder but the house was screened by trees and I contented myself with a glance at the houses round the other sides of the square— elegant, substantial and well cared for.

"And here we are."

I looked and was lost before we'd even left the car. The Beeches was a long, low house set back only slightly from the pavement with a sweep of immaculate gravel-swept drive in front of it. There was a small wing on each side.

17

"The vacant flat is the ground floor one in the right wing," Mr. Henry murmured, respecting my silence.

"How many flats are there altogether?"

"Eight; two up and two down in the main part of the house, one up and one down in each of the wings." He hesitated. "Would you like to see over it?"

"Yes, please."

Even if we had come to it first, I should have fallen for the Beeches, but after the disappointment of the other flats it was doubly attractive. As we walked over the crunching gravel I looked with approval at the gaily coloured window boxes, the four gleaming front doors close together in the angle of house and wing, which corresponded to those at the far end of the building. There were small wrought-iron balconies outside the long Georgian windows.

The door opened into a small hall and as Mr. Henry closed it behind us, the only light came from a round window in the wall opposite. Thick, emerald green carpet contrasted superbly with the white walls and woodwork. There were two doors on our left and two on the right.

"See what you think of this!" Mr. Henry flung open the nearer right-hand door with a flourish and my gasp of delight plainly satisfied him. It revealed a beautifully proportioned room with long windows giving onto the park, furnished elegantly in Regency style with brown and gold brocaded chairs and curtains and gleaming, slender-legged tables.

"It's—magnificent!" I said.

"The bedroom is the same length with the same outlook, but it's considerably narrower. It has an extra window at the

18

side of the house, but as you'll have noticed in the hall, not a lot of light comes in, as the beech trees grow rather near to the house. Let me show you."

Willingly I followed him, equally delighted with the long narrow bedroom and its elegant furniture.

"The bathroom and kitchen look over the gardens at the back." They were both small, compact and completely up-to-date. It was, of course, useless even to look at anywhere else, and now that his plan had succeeded, the avuncular Mr. Henry belatedly grew cautious on my behalf.

"I don't want to pressure you into anything that's beyond your means—"

"I can manage. In any case I must find a job. I just can't hang round here all day, and that will help. How soon can I move in?"

"Let me see. It won't take long. I'll have the agreement drawn up and then it will be necessary to go through the inventory with you. How would Saturday do?"

"Beautifully," I said happily.

"That's fine, then. I hope you'll be very happy here. We rather pride ourselves on Westhampton's peaceful, old-world atmosphere."

Mrs. Baillie had said much the same thing, but I'd had a narrow escape in the car and been on the receiving end of a rather sinister phone call, and I hadn't been here twenty-four hours yet. Pushing my mental reservations about Westhampton's peacefulness out of my mind, I followed Mr. Henry back to the car.

I returned to the George for lunch pleasantly elated at my good fortune, and remarked gaily to the receptionist, "I can fill in my address for you now—Flat 7, The Beeches, Park View, Westhampton!"

A man who had been standing at the noticeboard turned sharply and stared at me intently for a moment before moving away, and at once the uneasiness I had felt after the phone call returned in full measure. It had not been very wise to blurt out my new address so blithely. Suppose after all he had seen me leave the first estate agent's and been following me ever since? But that was surely ridiculous.

I decided that a drink before lunch might steady my jumping nerves and turned into the cocktail lounge. The man from the hall was seated at the bar and I felt his eyes watching me in the mirror as I made my way over to one of the tables against the wall. I gave my order to the hovering waiter and then looked defiantly across to meet the mirrored eyes. After a moment he looked away. He didn't seem unduly sinister after all, I reflected. He was immaculately dressed, with dark sleek hair and a thin clever face. Fleetingly I wondered if he could have been the driver of the Fiat. If so and it was outside in the car-park, I could rely on Jack to take action on my behalf, but it would hardly explain his apparent interest, since he would be as unlikely to recognize me from our last brief encounter as I would him.

My drink came and as I signed for it, my attention was caught by the somewhat precipitate arrival of a small, shabby man who paused just inside the doorway looking nervous and completely out of place in the comfortable opulence of the room. A moment later, to my intense surprise, he hurried over to the man at the bar and began to talk earnestly to him. Two less likely companions would have been hard to find, the

20

one so smooth and polished, the other so frayed and down at heel. Curiouser and curiouser.

My imagination was probably getting out of hand. I finished my drink and went through for lunch, illogically relieved when they did not appear and when I glanced into the bar on leaving the dining room, it was empty except for the waiter wiping over the tables.

The afternoon stretched blankly ahead. I moved over to the noticeboard hoping it might give times of local cinema performances, but my attention was caught instead by a small notice which read:

> Westhampton Little Theatre presents *An Inspector Calls* by J. B. Priestley. Thurs., 6th Sept.—Sat., 15th Sept. Doors open 7 P.M. Curtain rises 7.30. Matinee performances on Saturdays at 2.30.

"Where is the Little Theatre?" I asked the girl at the desk.

"Phoenix Street, Miss Durrell, the other side of town."

"How do I get there? I think I'll go and see if they've any seats left for this evening."

"I could phone through for you, but I doubt if they'll be—"

"No, thank you, I'd rather go myself. I've nothing to do this afternoon." And I didn't want to stay in the hotel in case I encountered the dark-eyed man again.

Armed with her directions, I set out, glad to have a destination in mind but cynically amused at the irresistible lure that the theatre—any theatre—still had for me. After Carl, it should have been the last place I'd make for, but my love for it went back further than my love for him. Even as a small child the cadence and rhythm of words had held me spellbound and after reading English with drama at university I had gone on to teach it at the exclusive Langland School for Girls. And there I might still happily have been had I not by chance met one of my fellow students who had opted for the stage and landed a small part in a West End production. She pressed a ticket on me and invited me backstage afterwards, and it was there, at an informal dressing-room party, that I had met Carl.

Carl had always resented what he referred to as my "scholastic background" and even in the early days there had been a note in his voice that wasn't wholly teasing when he referred, as he frequently did, to his "clever wife." Naturally, there had never been any question of my continuing to teach. "My God!" he'd protested in simulated horror. "Do you think I'd let it be known that I'm married to a schoolmarm?" In the total commitment of overwhelming love I had given it up without question, but now, for the first time, I was aware of buried resentment. It seemed unlikely that I could find a teaching job here in Westhampton without the rigmarole of writing to Langland for references, and in any case the autumn term had already begun.

By this time I had reached Phoenix Street, but a quick look up and down revealed no theatre that I could see. A woman was coming along trundling a basket on wheels and I stopped her to check my directions.

"Yes, that's right, it's down that little alley over there. See the notice?" And now that it was pointed out to me, I did in fact see the notice with the red arrow. Ruefully I thanked her and crossed the road. The word "theatre" was so firmly bound up in my mind with Carl and his lordly surroundings that it had not occurred to me that the one I was now seeking might be an inconspicuous little building "down the alley."

Even as I made my way over the uneven cobbles, I could see no sign of anything remotely resembling a theatre as I knew it. The approach was more that of some kind of warehouse—which, as it later turned out, was what the Little Theatre had once been. I turned into a mews-type courtyard surrounded on three sides by buildings, and on my immediate left a notice, once more repeating "Westhampton Little Theatre" to reassure its persevering clients, pointed directly up a steep flight of stairs.

Since the door at the bottom stood open, I went hesitantly up them. The walls on either side were hung with photographs of the company in previous productions: Joanna Lacy as Hedda Gabler, Laurence Grey and Leonard Beaufoy in a scene from *Julius Caesar.* A corridor ran across the top of the stairs, turning a corner almost immediately on the right and to the left widening into a foyer. But although there was a small bar at the far end, now firmly shuttered, and a box-office window alongside it, the place seemed deserted. I should, of course, have realized that the box office was unlikely to be open at three o'clock in the afternoon and let the hotel receptionist phone through for me later as she had no doubt been about to suggest.

I had actually turned to go when the sound of whistling reached me from behind the closed doors leading to the auditorium. Instinctively I moved towards them, and was

23

stretching out a hand to push them open when they swung suddenly towards me and a man in jeans and T-shirt, still whistling, came quickly through them, halting abruptly at the sight of me.

"Who are you? What are you doing here?" There was a note in his voice suggestive of alarm, which my presence hardly seemed to warrant.

"I'm sorry. I came to book a seat for this evening—"

"To book a seat?" He stood staring at me frowningly, drumming his fingers against the side of the mug he was holding.

"Yes, I'm sorry. I didn't realize the box office wouldn't be open. I'll come back later."

I turned away but he said more levelly, "Perhaps I can help. You must forgive me for being a bit abrupt; I thought I was alone in the building and you frightened the life out of me."

"I'm sorry," I said lamely, for the third time.

"I can see to it, anyway." He brushed past me and pushed open the door of the minute office. A seating plan of the theatre was spread out on the shelf beside the window.

"The seats are all one price. Where would you like to be?"

"About—the third row?" I said tentatively. Something about his manner made me slightly nervous.

"Row C, number nine. Just the one?"

"Just the one," I answered steadily.

"That'll be fifty pence."

I slid the coin across the shelf towards him and took the ticket in exchange. "Thank you. The door *was* open," I added, in a belated attempt at self-justification.

24

"Okay." He nodded briskly and slipped the money into the cash box, but for the second time within a few hours, I was acutely conscious of a pair of assessing eyes following me as I made my way back the length of the foyer until, thankfully, I turned down the stairs.

I emerged into Phoenix Street still somewhat nettled by my reception. Even accepting his explanation that my presence had startled him, I hadn't cared for his manner and I stupidly found myself wishing that I'd left the theatre before the sound of his whistling had made me aware of him.

I stopped abruptly and a wave of heat washed scaldingly over me as the piercing notes of that whistling echoed in my head. "Roses of Picardy." He had been whistling "Roses of Picardy." For a split second I couldn't pinpoint the reason for my panic reaction. Then I remembered: Picardy 127— wait till you hear the tune. This, surely, must be the tune the voice on the phone had been referring to. The possibility was a firm conviction to me. It was not as though the song were one of today's favourites; you could go for months without hearing it and then, twice in one day. Could it really be coincidence?

"Peaceful, olde-worlde Westhampton!" I thought with a bitter twist of humour. Was there, then, a connection between the phone call and the man at the theatre? And what possible link could there be anyway with a presumably respectable firm of estate agents? Was it all some elaborate sort of joke? I wished uselessly that I had never seen the name of Culpepper whatever it was, that I'd crossed the Avenue higher up and come first to kindly, concerned Mr. Henry. And suddenly a new dimension came into my loss of Carl—

25

the simple lack of someone with whom I could talk things over, whose advice I could ask. Yet, despairingly, I knew exactly what his reaction would be. "Forget it. The message wasn't meant for you in the first place, so what the hell!"

Easier said than done. On my way back to the hotel I passed a newsstand and on impulse bought a copy of the local evening paper. Once in my room, I spread it over the table and searched diligently for any report of a missing person, a kidnapping, anything that might tie in with what I had overheard. There was nothing. It might, of course, be too soon; the note, whatever it was, was only being delivered today. I resolved to listen to the news summary before going down for my early dinner, and in the meantime searched out the garage attendant to enquire about the progress on my car.

"There you are, miss," he said proudly. "Good as new! I was able to match it up a treat!"

"That's marvellous," I said gratefully, running my hand affectionately along the bodywork. I would not have fancied having to find my way home in the dark after the evening performance. My present state of wary apprehension would have detected an assailant in every shadowed doorway.

"Jack," I said impulsively, "I wonder if you can help me —you must know Westhampton pretty well."

"Like the back of me hand, miss."

"Do you happen to know where—where Picardy Street is?" I held my breath, my hand pressed down on the metal of the car absorbing its coldness.

"Picardy Street?" he repeated. "No, I can't say I've heard of that one. Hereabouts, is it?"

26

"I think so. Could it be Picardy Road, or Lane, or anything? A friend of mine was staying there but I can't remember the exact address."

"No, miss, there's no Picardy Street that I know of, nor anything like it where any friend of yours might be." He looked at me curiously.

"Oh, well, I must have misheard it. Never mind." I pushed myself away from the car and went back upstairs. It was now just twenty-four hours since my arrival in Westhampton, and they had certainly been full of incident. Momentarily, before my mental censorship swung into action, I wondered what Carl was doing, whether he was anxious about me or merely glad to have me out of the way. Bleakly, I accepted that there was no way of finding out.

Chapter 3

I DISCOVERED to my slight dismay that it was not, in fact, possible to park very near the theatre, and a certain length of dark streets would have to be negotiated after all. However, it was still almost daylight as I locked the car door just after seven-fifteen and made my way back to Phoenix Street.

The atmosphere at the theatre was very different from the deserted barracks it had appeared that afternoon. The small foyer was filled to overflowing with laughing, talking groups of people and a girl with a tray of empty coffee cups was trying to thread her way between them.

"Any more coffee, Kitty?" someone called, and she paused for a moment.

"Sorry, we're rather hard-pressed this evening. Can you possibly wait till the interval?"

"Right-o, I'll make do with a whisky!"

Going to the theatre alone was something I was used to. Even after our marriage, Carl was more likely to be on stage than beside me in the auditorium, and often when I saw plays he was neither appearing in nor producing, he would be busily engaged in those activities elsewhere. Nevertheless, I did feel rather an odd-man-out here, where everyone seemed to know each other, and since there was no chance of a coffee, I moved through into the auditorium, buying a program on the way.

The theatre was tiny, prettily decorated in white and gold, with the traditional red plush seats. At a quick reckoning I estimated it would seat a hundred and twenty at the most. Several people were already in their seats and a man with glasses was playing the piano in the minute orchestra pit. I found my place in the third row, sat down and opened the program. Some of the names I recognized from the photographs on the staircase: Leonard Beaufoy, Marion Dobie, Robert Harling— I paused, trying to probe the chord the last name had struck in my memory. I had heard it before today. And obediently the memory resolved itself into Carl's voice, some weeks ago: "There's a bloke I've been hearing a lot about lately, Robert Harling. He's in rep. or something at Westhampton. He might be a possible Clarence to my Richard."

Which memory also served to solve the question of where I had heard Westhampton mentioned recently. Had I been able to pinpoint its association when Mrs. Baillie had first mentioned it, I should probably have gone farther afield, at least after the first night, rather than stay in any place that had the remotest connection with Carl. Now, having settled for the Beeches, it was too late and in any case I liked the town. I could hardly go through life avoiding any place Carl had ever referred to.

Out in the foyer a bell rang and the crowds began to filter

through. With a perfunctory little bow the pianist took his leave to a sprinkling of applause and with the mounting excitement such a moment never failed to bring, I sat back and waited for the curtain to go up.

The set, although not as opulent as those at the Playhouse, was pleasant and effective and it was clear within the first few minutes that the acting was of a high standard. It was no great surprise to recognize among the actors the man I had spoken to that afternoon; he was playing the part of Eric, the son of the family. I checked his name on the program and found it to be Stephen Darby. Several times in those first few minutes I was a little disconcerted to find his eyes speculatively on me, and my initial sense of antipathy strengthened. I was careful not to look at him throughout the rest of the first act.

The curtain came down, the lights went up, and I made my way with the others out to the foyer in search of coffee. The signs were not too hopeful. There was a long queue already at a hatch opening onto what looked like a kitchenette and I could see the girl who'd passed me before, cheeks hot and flustered, pouring into cups set out on a tray while behind her a kettle was boiling uproariously. It looked very much as though she were in need of assistance. I threaded my way past the queue and out of the foyer into the passage leading to the stairs. Just short of them and directly opposite the cloakroom was the door I was looking for. I tapped on it, went in and found myself in the steam-filled room. The girl turned distractedly towards me.

"Can I help?"

"Oh, bless you!" she exclaimed fervently. "Could you see

to that infernal kettle and fill up the coffeepots waiting on the side? There's more milk under the sink."

Without more ado I set to work making the coffee, pouring it into the never-ending succession of empty cups, replenishing milk jugs and sugar basins. At last the queue in front of us shortened and dwindled away and I was able to pour out a cup for myself. The girl called Kitty came back and joined me.

"You are an angel; thank you so much! I was nearly going scatty! There should be two of us, but the girl who's usually on with me has sprained her wrist."

"Glad I could help. Is it your regular job to do the coffee?"

"No, we take it in turns, along with the bar duty and program-selling."

"We?" I queried.

She looked surprised. "The members."

"Is this a theatre club? I'd no idea! I'm afraid I'm an interloper, then."

She smiled. "Are you? They usually check up when they issue tickets."

"Well, I came along this afternoon on the offchance and one of the actors booked my seat for me."

"Ah. I suppose it never occurred to him to ask you. Anyway, the sub's only a pound a year."

"Then I'd better make an honest woman of myself and join straight away."

"You haven't time now, there's the bell. Thanks again for your help. By the way, my name's Kitty Fulton."

"Ginnie Durrell. Shall I help out again in the second interval?"

She dimpled. "I didn't like to ask, but I was hoping you would!"

I had only just regained my seat when the curtain went up and the play reached out for me again. Knowing it so well, I found myself assessing the acting ability of the cast with a more or less professional eye, imagining Carl's pungent comments on their various capabilities. Laurence Grey, who played the Inspector, had also directed the play, I noticed, and I wondered whether Suzanne Grey, in the part of Sheila, was his wife. She was a striking-looking girl with sleek, straight black hair curving smoothly onto her face and long legs with fragile ankles like a thoroughbred racehorse. She acted with a staccato kind of nervousness which admirably suited the part; even when she was in the background, the air of tension was kept up by the restless twisting and pulling of her fingers. It was so authentic a performance that I found myself wondering unaccountably whether any part of it was real.

The second interval came and I quickly made my way back to Kitty. This time the queue was not so long, most people seeming to be thronging round the bar, and we were able to talk more.

"Look, I know this is an awful cheek," Kitty began awkwardly, "but is there any chance at all of your coming to help tomorrow and Saturday? I feel awful asking you, but—"

"I don't see why not," I said slowly. I had not been looking forward to the prospect of spending another evening at the hotel before I could move into my flat, and this seemed a pleasant alternative. As far as Saturday was concerned, with only two suitcases to my name, the moving-in operation would not be a major undertaking. And not least, even this humble task was associated with the theatre, which had always been meat and drink to me. Only later did I wonder whether my curiosity to learn more about Stephen Darby and the tune he had been whistling had also weighed in my acceptance.

"You would?" Kitty eagerly tossed back her long brown hair. "Rachel won't be back this week and it's the last night on Saturday. It would make all the difference if I could count on you being here."

"Okay, count away! Does the place close down next week?"

"Only to the public. They start rehearsing in earnest for the next play which opens in three weeks' time."

"How many productions do they do a year?"

"Eight or nine, I think. This is the first one after the summer break. The theatre closes from the end of June till September."

The bell sounded and I left Kitty to the collecting and washing-up of the coffee cups in which for the next two evenings I would be assisting her.

The last act played itself out with admirably mounting tension and I experienced the usual thrill of unease even though I knew the ending. It had been a most enjoyable performance.

I paused at the box office to request a membership form and duly filled it in and handed over my pound. There was no sign of Kitty and the hatch was closed. No doubt she had cleared up and gone home. I made my way slowly down the steep stairs after the last of the departing playgoers, my

33

footsteps quickening as I turned perforce into the less well-lighted streets where I had left the car. After the warmth and companionship of the brightly lit theatre the streets seemed extra cold and dark, and I thought of the rest of the audience, their fears and anxieties perhaps reclaiming them after the brief respite of the make-believe we had shared, separating now and going home through the dark.

It was with a feeling of melancholy as well as relief that I reached the car and let myself in and, closing my mind to everything but the physical act of driving, I hurriedly made my way back to the hotel.

After breakfast the next morning there was a phone call from Mr. Henry asking me to go round to his office to sign the tenancy agreement, after which we could go on to the flat and check the inventory.

Westhampton in the sunshine looked as peaceful as ever as I drove through the busy streets to the Avenue. I cruised slowly past the window of Culpepper's and saw a middle-aged woman standing at the telephone. Had the message I'd received been intended for her? There had still been no report either in the paper or on the radio of anything remotely connected with what I'd overheard. In fact, if it hadn't been for Stephen Darby's whistling and his subsequent rather surreptitious watching of me, I might well have decided to forget the whole thing. As it was, with nothing better to occupy my mind, I continued to circle round it.

The agreement was straightforward and it was with a pleasant sense of at least temporary ownership that I returned with Mr. Henry to the Beeches. An elderly woman was letting herself into one of the other flats as we arrived, and she nodded briefly at us. Inside Number 7 we went meticulously through every pan and every teaspoon, every blanket and ornament. I was full of impatience to be here alone, hanging my clothes in the wardrobe, making myself some tea and being able to relax in private. The only faint shadow on my anticipation was the remembrance of having carelessly blurted out my future whereabouts and thereby aroused such apparent interest in the dark-eyed man at the hotel.

I spent half an hour after lunch happily making out a basic list of necessities to take with me the next day, and the rest of the afternoon in buying them.

That evening I dined early again in the almost deserted dining room and once more drove to the theatre, this time to report for duty. By the time the doors opened at seven, Kitty and I were ready for the invasion.

The evening passed quickly. As soon as we'd finished washing and drying the pre-show cups and saucers, it was time to fill the urn for the interval coffee, keeping the kettle going for topping-up operations. And when we'd washed those cups, the second interval was already looming. No wonder Kitty had been flustered on her own.

It was during the final act that the door of the kitchenette burst open unceremoniously and Stephen Darby looked in.

"Kitty, have you got—"

He broke off as his eyes fell on me, and I was sure the same wariness was back in them as I had noticed when he had come upon me in the empty theatre. "Hello," he said slowly. "You here again?"

"Ginnie's being an angel and helping out while Rachel's off. What did you want, Steve?"

"I was going to ask if you'd such a thing as an aspirin.

Suzanne has a raging headache. She's jittery enough at the moment—" He broke off abruptly, as though regretting he had said so much.

"Sorry, I hardly ever use them. Can you help, Ginnie?"

I said steadily, "I might have a couple in my bag. Just a minute." I went to the shelf where I'd left it and retrieved a bottle with only a few tablets in it. I handed it to Stephen Darby, my eyes meeting his with forced calm. "She can have these if they're any use."

"Thanks," he said briefly. His eyes raked my face for a moment, then he was gone.

"Do you know Steve?" Kitty asked curiously.

"It was he who gave me my ticket yesterday afternoon."

"Oh, I see."

And he wasn't pleased to see me here again. Why? Thoughtfully I picked up the discarded tea towel and went on drying the cups.

The following morning I awoke with a sense of excitement. Immediately after breakfast I collected the few things I'd unpacked so miserably on Wednesday evening and put them back in the cases. Then, while the porter carried them out to the car, I went to the desk to pay my bill. As luck would have it, Mrs. Baillie was there.

"I hear you've found yourself somewhere to live," she said pleasantly. "I'm so glad. Do call in from time to time and let us know how you're getting on. I feel a certain responsibility for you, after all!"

"Thank you, I will. You must come and have coffee with me one morning."

I drove first to the estate agents to collect the keys and

then, feeling happier than I had for days, straight to the Beeches. Mr. Henry had shown me the garage that would be mine the previous day, but I parked the car by the front door while I unloaded the suitcases and provisions and carried them inside. In any case, I would be needing the car for the theatre that evening and was also quite likely to discover some necessity I'd forgotten which would mean a dash to the shops before they closed. The milk I had ordered stood waiting on the step and the newspaper was in the letter box. I dumped them with the boxes of groceries on the kitchen table and went back to shut the boot. On my way in again I paused to glance quickly at the cards under the bells by the three front doors close to mine. The one alongside my own, belonging to the flat above me, read in neatly printed capitals: MISS P. DAVIS, MISS S. BRIGG. Of the two nearest flats in the main building, the ground floor apparently housed Colonel and Mrs. Bligh and the one above them, a Mr. M. M. Sinclair. Idly I wondered whether I would have any point of contact with my new neighbours. I was not long kept in doubt.

For the remainder of the morning I pottered happily round the flat putting away the things I had bought, unpacking my suitcases and generally congratulating myself on my good fortune in having found myself somewhere so pleasant. In the minute kitchen every inch was utilized to the most advantage. There was even a small dishwasher, fitted neatly beneath the sink, though I doubted whether I should ever collect enough dirty crockery to justify switching it on. The window overlooked the sweeping lawns and huge trees at the back of the house and as I watched a squirrel raced across

37

the grass, its tail streaming out behind it like a feathered banner. Mr. Henry had explained that the gardens were shared between all the flats, whose owners paid a nominal sum for them to be kept in order. Perhaps I would go and relax out there this afternoon.

I had a hasty lunch of bread, cheese and coffee and then went through to the drawing room. The Hodgsons who owned the flat certainly had exquisite taste. All the books on the long, low shelves were finished beautifully in morocco, hide and suede with gold-tooled lettering. The heavy curtains which, I discovered, closed with a smooth swish on the pulling of a cord, were of a brown and gold brocade almost identical with the upholstery of the easy chairs, while the sofa and small chaise-longue were covered respectively in brown and gold velvet. The windows were Georgian style sashes, and one of them opened just far enough to enable me to climb out onto the tiny wrought-iron balcony. I stood there for a moment, leaning on the rail and looking out across the autumn tints of the foliage in the park opposite. No doubt these balconies were supposed to be merely ornamental; the little pots of gaily coloured plants could easily be reached by leaning out of the window with the long-spouted watering can I had found in the kitchen.

"Hello there!"

I turned sharply to see a girl in a trouser suit coming across the gravel. "Have you just moved in? I saw the car and wondered if you wanted any help?"

"That's very kind of you. If you'll wait a moment, I'll climb back inside and let you in!"

Feeling rather foolish, I crawled back into the drawing

38

room and reached the front door at the same time as she did. She smiled and held out a hand.

"I'm Sarah Foss, from Number Two, over in the other wing."

"Ginnie Durrell. Do come in."

"I say, this is swish, isn't it?" she said admiringly, following me into the drawing room. "I've never been in here before. I don't mind telling you our flat doesn't come up to this standard!"

I laughed. "Isn't it gorgeous? I'm rather afraid to touch anything."

"How long have you taken it for?"

"Six months, but I believe there's a possibility of the lease being extended if the Hodgsons decide to stay out there for longer." I closed my mind to the implications of so long an absence from Carl and added hastily, "Are you renting, too?"

"No, Andrew and I bought our flat when we were married three years ago. Needless to say, it wasn't nearly as expensive then as it would be now. Where have you come from?"

"London."

"You'll find it very different here!"

"Yes, but I like it very much."

"Have you got a job?" She coloured a little and laughed shamefacedly. "Am I being rude? Andrew always says I'm too inquisitive!"

"It doesn't matter. I haven't a job at the moment, but I must get one if I want to keep up with the rent!"

"There are usually quite a lot of secretarial jobs going, if that's your line." She looked round the room. "You're remarkably well organized considering you only moved in this morning! Not a tea chest in sight!"

"Actually I didn't bring very much with me."

"Oh?" She waited hopefully but there I wasn't prepared to help her. "Would you like a cup of tea?"

"Love one, but I mustn't be too long. Andrew's up a ladder decorating the loo and I promised I'd be back soon." She followed me through into the kitchen. "Actually, one reason I came was to ask if you'd like to come round for drinks at lunch time tomorrow? I'll invite some of the other inmates, so you can weigh us all up!"

I smiled, filling the kettle. "Are they as bad as that?"

She perched on a corner of the table. "Well, they can roughly be divided into three parts, like Caesar's Gaul. There's the Oldies—Miss Cavendish and the Blighs. Then there's the Lily-white Boys—"

"The what?" I queried incredulously.

"A couple of rather beaut young men in Number Four. Photographers or something. And thirdly, there's Us, i.e., Andy and I, Moira Francis and the kids, and Pam and Stephanie, who live above you. Unfortunately they're still away on holiday. And lastly, in no category but strictly on his own, is 'M.M.' "

"And who might he be?"

"M. M. Sinclair. I swear it stands for Mystery Man. He's a kind of cat-that-walks-by-himself. No one knows what he does or where he came from, or anything."

"How frustrating for you!"

She grinned. "It didn't take you long to sum me up, did it? Anyway, I'll invite them all, but I don't suppose he'll

40

come. He doesn't strike me as being very sociably minded."

I opened three cupboards before I found the teacups. "It's very kind of you to go to all this trouble on my account."

"Nonsense, it's time we had a party, anyway. You'll sort them all out in time. The odd-numbered flats are ground-floor and the even upstairs—no doubt you've already gathered that. The Oldies have ground-floor ones because they don't like stairs, but they don't like noise either, which makes life hard for those above them. Miss Cavendish is always sending frigid little notes upstairs to the boys. She's a retired headmistress, so you can imagine!" Sarah sipped at the hot tea but it didn't interrupt her flow. "Mind you, the Blighs are better off now M.M.'s above them. I bet he doesn't make a *sound,* creeping around up there."

"Presumably he has a dark cloak and a false beard?"

"You may well laugh," she said darkly, "but there's something odd about him. He doesn't seem to have a regular job, for one thing, he's in and out all day. Perhaps he's a Private Eye or something like that."

"Rather an upper-class one, to come to roost here." I forbore from commenting that if the mysterious Mr. Sinclair were really an investigator of some kind, he could do a lot worse than solicit Sarah's help.

She finished her tea and stood up, tugging down her jacket. "I'd better go and start on the groundwork by phoning them all. See you tomorrow, about twelve." And with a nonchalant wave of her hand, she was gone.

The sun had gone in and I changed my mind about going into the garden, relaxing with my book instead on the comfortable sofa. I watched the early news on television—still no

41

reports of a kidnapping—and then went through to grill my solitary pork chop. It didn't feel like Saturday at all; this time last week we'd been preparing for the Winthrops' party. I remembered bleakly that Leonie had been there, playing up to Carl as usual. If I hadn't happened to go unexpectedly to the theatre on Wednesday, I would have given her attentions no more serious consideration than anyone else's.

I wrenched my mind away from the abyss of self-pity yawning in front of me and instead forced myself to repeat the words of the telephone call, and suddenly a fact I had not registered before struck me for the first time. The voice had been wrong, somehow out of character for the pseudo-criminal slang it had been using. It had, in fact, been a particularly pleasant voice, well-modulated and resonant. It could even have been a trained voice—an actor's voice.

Carefully I pushed the uneaten chop to the edge of my plate and laid down my knife and fork. That, of course, would tie in with the whistling, but it was all so wildly circumstantial that I couldn't give the idea much credence.

When I joined Kitty in the kitchenette an hour or so later, the working surfaces where last night I had laid out the coffeecups were covered with a profusion of paper bags.

"What's all this?" I asked curiously.

"Oh, savouries and things. We can see to them after the second interval."

"Savouries? What for?"

She turned to look at me. "Didn't I tell you? We always have a small celebration after the last performance."

"The actors, you mean?"

"Yes, they come through here when the audience has left.

42

You'll stay, won't you? It won't go on for very long, but it's usually good fun."

"Oh yes," I said slowly, "I'll stay."

Accordingly, after clearing away the crockery after the second interval, Kitty and I embarked on decorating savoury biscuits with different toppings, chopping up celery and filling it with cream cheese, tipping out packets of salted nuts and jars of olives. "We can put away the cups and saucers, anyway. They won't be wanting coffee!" Kitty said.

As it turned out, it was quite a sizable party, since besides the small cast several other actors and actresses, some of whose photographs decorated the stairway, came to join in the celebration. Kitty and I were kept busy for a while handing round the trays of canapés, but it wasn't long before Stephen Darby made his way over to me. With great deliberation he selected a savoury from the plate I held.

"You're Ginnie Durrell, I believe?" So he had asked Kitty about me.

"I am," I replied steadily.

"Are you given to good works of this nature?"

"I hardly think what I'm doing warrants that definition, but Kitty was short-handed and I enjoy being at the theatre."

He raised one eyebrow. "Stage-struck, Miss Durrell?"

I flushed with annoyance. "In a manner of speaking. I read drama at university."

"I *beg* your pardon! Suzanne—" He put one arm out to encircle the waist of the girl who was passing. "This is the young lady who kindly supplied your aspirins last night. You'll be even more grateful, I'm sure, when you hear she's a university graduate!"

Suzanne Grey was tall, her skin flawless, her eyes an unusually dark grey. She looked as highly strung and edgy as she had on stage, and she certainly wasn't acting now. To my relief she didn't seem to have taken in Stephen's last comment.

"It was very kind of you. I had the most diabolical headache."

Stephen Darby's eyes were still on my face. "I don't remember seeing you before this week. Have you lived in Westhampton long?"

"No, only since Wednesday, as a matter of fact."

"Wednesday? And it must have been—what?—Thursday afternoon you came here? You certainly didn't waste much time, did you?"

I said stiffly, "I told you I've always been interested in the theatre."

"But mainly from the other side of the footlights, I imagine."

His careless superiority stung me into lack of caution. "Not always, by any means. Quite a few of my friends are professional actors."

"Oh? Who are they?"

Too late I realized the trap I'd laid for myself. I had no intention of betraying my connection with Carl. "I don't suppose you'll have heard of any of them," I lied quickly. "People who were at university with me."

He laughed shortly. "From the way you were talking, I was beginning to think you were on nodding terms with Alec Guinness and Carl Clements!"

"Will you excuse me?" I said clearly. "I think Kitty wants

44

some more help." I pushed my way blindly through the crowd over to the hatch. Behind me a slightly amused voice said, "Has Steve been riling you? Don't take any notice of him!"

I turned to find Robert Harling behind me.

"What was all that about Carl Clements? Do you know him?"

I drew a deep breath. "I have met him," I said.

"God, I'd give my right arm for a chance to act with him! They say he's a bastard to work with, but who cares?" He leaned past me to put a plate down on the counter. "You're new here, aren't you?"

"Yes, Ginnie Durrell." If I repeated the name much more, I'd forget I'd ever been Ginnie Clements.

"Did you see the play?"

"Yes, I enjoyed it very much."

"A bit dated, perhaps, but of course it was even when it was written. We must seem small fish to you here, if you're used to the West End."

"I didn't say—" I began desperately, but someone else had attracted his attention and my disclaimer hung on the air. I turned back to the counter and began mechanically to load more plates of assorted savouries onto a tray, but my rather agitated thoughts were interrupted as Suzanne Grey's voice rose stridently above the low hum of conversation.

"For God's sake, Laurence, will you drop it? I don't know, I tell you!"

There was a fractional pause, then a more concentrated noise as everyone quickly started talking again at the same time. I had picked up the tray and started back into the

45

throng when without warning Suzanne spun away from her husband's restraining hand and cannoned into me.

"How the hell can I stop it if I don't know what you're talking about? Stop being so bloody superior!" And with two angry spots of colour high on her cheeks, she pushed her way between the chattering groups and went clattering down the stairs. Another theatrical marriage on the rocks, I thought achingly. Stephen put a hand on Laurence Grey's arm. "She's been under a considerable strain, don't forget," he said in a low voice. "Can't you suggest she goes away for a while? She's not in the next production, is she?"

"You know damn well she wouldn't hear of it," Laurence replied. "Not while she thinks there's the remotest chance of — God, Stephen, I don't know if I can go through with it."

The quick, low-voiced exchange had only taken a couple of seconds and it seemed to be imperative that Stephen at least should not realize I had overheard it. Although I had no idea what they were talking about, the tone of their voices had implied something private, even secretive, and Stephen was already suspicious of my continuing presence at the theatre. To my relief I had managed to put a respectable distance between them and myself before they turned.

By midnight I had had more than enough of the party and Kitty caught my surreptitious glance at my watch. "Tired, Ginnie? Then you go home. Liz will help me tidy up when they've gone." She indicated the girl beside her, who had taken the part of the maid in the play. "Anyway, we've no washing-up to do, the bar crew will take care of the glasses."

"If you're sure, then." I was suddenly longing for the elegant privacy of my narrow bedroom at the Beeches.

"Thanks again for all you've done and if you're passing any time during the next three weeks, there'll always be coffee on hand during rehearsals. You can even sit in the back stalls and watch if you like!"

"I'll remember," I promised, but at the moment I had had enough of the theatre and its strains and stresses. The night air was cool after the heat in the foyer and I wrapped my coat round me as I hurried through the dark streets to the car.

I was a little apprehensive of my first drive in the dark to Park View, but I took only one wrong turn before I found myself turning into the square. Only one street lamp at each corner was lighted and the park huddled in the centre, a black, impenetrable space of whispering leaves and moving grasses. I drove round it as quickly as possible, one side, two, three, and into the driveway of the Beeches. The only light in the entire building was in the window of Number 6. The Mystery Man burning his midnight oil, I thought. How the knowledge would have gratified Sarah!

I went carefully down the rather narrow space alongside the west wing to the row of garages behind. Alongside them lay the dark reaches of the sleeping garden. An owl hooted suddenly, bringing my heart to my throat. Hurriedly, fumblingly, I pushed the key into the garage door, swung it up and over and drove in. It was ridiculous, I told myself scathingly, to give way to this primeval fear of the dark. Nevertheless, I should try to bring a torch with me next time I was out at night. Wishing fervently that the garages were at my own end of the building, I stumbled back past the west wing and along the front of the house, my footsteps sounding unnaturally loud on the gravel, and with a sigh of relief inserted the key in my own front door. As I did so, I happened to glance up and with a shock of alarm saw a tall figure motionless against the lighted window above. My shredded nerves disintegrated at once and I hurled myself inside and slammed and bolted the door. No doubt, I told myself sternly as I hurriedly drew the curtains in bedroom and bathroom, he had merely looked out to find the source of the footsteps. After all, why should Sarah's Mystery Man care what time I arrived home?

I washed and undressed in the same mindless haste, climbed into bed, pulled the blankets up to my ears and, thankfully, slept.

Chapter 4

IT was nearly ten o'clock when I woke the next morning. For a while I lay luxuriously in the wide bed, going over the party of the night before: Suzanne's outburst and her husband's hurried exchange with Stephen Darby. She wouldn't go away while she thought there was the remotest chance of—what? It could be a hundred things, but it was another small question mark, whether or not it had any bearing on the one that had been puzzling me during the last few days.

I climbed out of bed at last and drew back the curtains from the side window. Barely six feet away the row of rustling beech trees edged the narrow path which led round to my own back door and the garden. Under the canopy of their branches the gravel was dark with heavy dew.

I had a leisurely bath followed by a brunch of coffee and scrambled eggs to lay a necessary foundation for Sarah's drinks. I had eaten little the night before, only a mouthful or so of the chop and a few biscuits at the theatre. At twelve o'clock, with a final appraising look in the long mirror, I picked up my bag and set out for the party. Sarah's front door stood open and a notice was pinned to the newel post of the staircase just inside: "Come on up!"

Typically Sarah, I thought with a smile as I complied. I could hear her voice as I reached the top of the stairs. There was a small hall similar to my own and through the open door of the drawing room I could see Sarah herself cheerfully dispensing some suspicious-looking liquid from a glass jug.

"Ginnie, hello! Come in. Meet Moira Francis from downstairs, and Roger and Michael."

I smiled across at the tall, fair-haired woman and the two boys and turned as Andrew Foss came into the room and was introduced in his turn.

"I believe you have the flat corresponding to ours in the other wing," Moira Francis said.

"That's right, all to myself!"

"I imagine it would be ideal for one or two, but it's a bit of a squash for three, especially when two of them are great, clumsy boys!" She looked fondly at her sons. "We've divided the bedroom in two, of course. With the second window it adapts very well, and I have the front half."

"There are just the three of you?"

"Yes, my husband died ten years ago, when the boys were small."

"I'm sorry," I said inadequately. More people were coming into the room and Sarah brought them over in turn to meet me—Miss Cavendish, whom I had seen going into her flat when I'd called with Mr. Henry, a small, birdlike woman with grey hair and sharp eyes; the Lily-white Boys, to wit Robin Kershaw and Donald King, immaculate in dove-grey suits with large floppy ties and carefully waved hair; the Colonel and his lady straight from the pages of Somerset Maugham, he red-faced and silver-haired with a neat, military moustache, she clinging to a faded prettiness. I was marvelling at their closeness to prototype when, across Mrs. Bligh's fragile bent shoulder I saw the last guest enter the room—Sarah's Mystery Man. And as our eyes met, I bit my lip to hold back a startled exclamation. It was the man who had paid me such marked attention at the hotel. Dutifully Sarah brought him across. She was saying, "I'm not sure if you know anyone here, Mr. Sinclair, but may I start by introducing Colonel and Mrs. Bligh, and Miss Ginnie Durrell."

I caught the quick, instantly suppressed flicker of surprise that crossed his face. Had he thought I was someone else? His hand was hard and horny, his clasp firm. "I believe I saw —Miss Durrell last week, at the George," he said smoothly. "How do you do? Colonel—"

I moved over to rejoin Moira Francis, who was hemmed in a corner with the photographers, my mind racing to collate this latest development, but before I had made any progress Mr. Sinclair followed me over.

"I hope my appearance wasn't too unpleasant a shock," he murmured in my ear. "Your jaw dropped a good three inches!"

"I'm sorry. I was just—"

"Admittedly I had the advantage over you. I overheard you giving your address at the hotel, and when Mrs. Foss invited me round 'to welcome a new neighbour,' I knew of course whom to expect." He paused. "I'm afraid I may have startled you last night, at the window."

196185

I flushed, remembering my headlong flight. "Not really, but I was still recovering from feeling my way round from the garage, and to look up and see a figure silhouetted—"

"My apologies; I was just closing the window." He lifted one eyebrow in a way that reminded me of Stephen Darby at his most sardonic. "Are you afraid of the dark then, Miss Durrell?" Again the slight hesitation over my name as his eyes went thoughtfully to the hand with which I was holding my glass. I followed their direction and saw to my confusion that there was still a clear, white band round my finger where Carl's ring had been.

Defiantly I raised my eyes to his. It was no damn business of his what I chose to call myself. In the meantime his lazy question still hung on the air between us.

"Not exactly afraid, " I answered crisply, "but I do prefer to be able to see what I'm doing, not to mention what other people are!"

He gave a short laugh. "Point taken. But if you're really nervous about parking your car at night, I'd be pleased to do it for you."

I looked at him for a moment but his eyes met mine blandly, innocently.

"That's very kind," I said at last, "but I don't intend to be out late again for a while." I turned back to the group beside us.

"I'm afraid I couldn't afford your prices, Donald!" Moira Francis was saying with a smile.

"But, my dear, I'm sure we could come to an arrangement, especially for a friend. It would be a pleasure. We used to consider ourselves quite exclusive, but the people who have the money nowadays, you just wouldn't believe!" He turned

52

to his companion. "Did I tell you, duckie, that Mr. Bruce phoned about the proofs? And you'll never begin to guess where we're to send them! To the Picardy!"

My hand jerked out of control and the drink spilled down my dress. I was hardly aware of Mr. Sinclair's exclamation, though I took the clean handkerchief he handed me and automatically dabbed at my skirt. Robin Kershaw was still marvelling at this piece of news, so it didn't seem too inappropriate to enquire a little shakily, "The Picardy? What's that?"

His eyes, limpid, grey and long-lashed, flickered in my direction. "My dear, the most ghastly place! A sleazy hotel out on the Amesbury road." He giggled. "The kind of place where most rooms are let by the hour, if you know what I mean. You can imagine the shock it was—the girl whose portrait we took was supposed to be his daughter!"

My head was spinning. A hotel. Then 127 would be the room number. I remembered Jack's reply in the hotel garage. "There's no Picardy *Street* that I know of, nor anything like it where any friend of yours might be." No doubt he knew of the Picardy Hotel and its unsavoury reputation but it would not have occurred to him that that was the place I was enquiring about. And the phone call. Could it have been *"the* Picardy" and "Room" 127? It was possible—he'd been speaking so rapidly and I was straining to grasp the overall information rather than individual words. It was a lead, anyway, the first I'd had. What could I do about it?

". . . Miss Durrell?"

Hastily I dragged my thoughts back to Mr. Sinclair. "I beg your pardon?"

"I said if you let me have your glass I'll get it refilled for you." He was watching me closely, his eyes full of curiosity.

"Oh, thank you. And for the hanky. I'll wash it out and let you have it back."

"Nonsense." He took it firmly out of my hand and put it in his pocket. Somehow I managed to make light conversation for another half hour or so until the guests began to leave.

"Thank you so much, Sarah," I said sincerely. "I feel much more at home now. You and Andy must come over to me one evening."

"We'd love to. See you soon, anyway." Her eyes darted to Mr. Sinclair at my side and she gave me a swift, concealed wink. He walked back the length of the house with me to our respective front doors.

"Don't forget what I said about parking the car."

"Thank you, I won't. Goodbye, Mr. Sinclair."

"The name's Marcus." His finger moved along the printed card by his bell. "Marcus Montgomery Sinclair. How about that?"

I smiled involuntarily. "Sarah thought the initials stood for Mystery Man."

"Really? I'd no idea I'd excited such interest!"

Before I could think of a suitably crushing retort, he had gone. Back in my own flat I moved restlessly up and down the drawing room. It was no good. I'd have to go along to the Picardy, just to have a look at it. Even such an unsalubrious place should be reasonably innocuous on a Sunday afternoon. I went quickly to the bedroom, collected headscarf and sunglasses with some half-formed idea of disguise, and let myself silently out of the flat. I glanced apprehensively up at

Marcus's window but no one appeared. I walked swiftly back the way I had just come and round the corner of the building. Andy and Sarah's front door still stood open and I could imagine them upstairs washing glasses and ashtrays. The garage door swung up and over and a moment later I was driving out of the square and along Grove Street. A quick glance at my Esso map had given me the number of the Amesbury road.

After a while I found myself among the dingier suburbs where Mr. Henry had reluctantly taken me last Thursday. The farther I went, the more run-down the houses became. Front doors opening onto the street stood ajar, revealing dark hallways with torn linoleum and occasionally children played on the doorstep. The heat hung like a blanket over the town, a thousand dust motes caught in the rays of sunshine.

I drew in to a garage at the side of the road to fill up with petrol. "Could you tell me where the Picardy Hotel is?" I asked the attendant offhandedly.

"Certainly, miss." There was a leer in his voice which brought the colour to my face. "Half a mile along there, on the right. Opposite what used to be the Roxy Cinema and is now a bingo hall."

"Thank you," I said carefully.

"Have a good time!"

With burning cheeks I put my foot down and shot back onto the road, hearing him laugh. I asked for that, I told myself, but it was unavoidable, I'd had to check I was on the right road. And here, after all my wondering, was the Picardy at last, a dreary-looking place with a frontage of dirty windows set into the yellow brickwork. For a moment a strong urge for self-protection almost made me drive past. But I knew I'd never rest until I'd made some enquiries which might shed some light on that cryptic message I'd unwillingly received. As I sat in the car trying to summon up the courage to go in, a coloured man went up the steps with a girl clinging to his arm. I gave them a chance to get clear of the hallway, then I tied the scarf round my head, locked the car and quickly crossed the road.

It was the smell I noticed first, of stale food, dusty heat and dogs. The hall carpet was threadbare and there was the distant sound of a vacuum cleaner. Behind the desk a pale, untidy woman was reading *The News of the World.* Cautiously I moved towards her.

"Yes, dear?" she said without looking up. "Want a room?"

"I—no, thank you. I was wondering if you could help me."

She looked up then. "Not if you've come to ask questions, dearie. More than my job's worth."

"Not really, no, but I'm worried about my friend—a gentleman who was here last week."

"Oh?" Her little eyes were trying to penetrate my sunglasses.

"I—think he was in Room 127."

"Not 127 again! You the young lady what was looking for him on Friday? Can't tell you any more than I did then. He went off with his friend and later the other young gentleman came back to pay the bill and collect the cases. I've seen nothing of either of them since."

"He—didn't leave any forwarding address?" I persisted, and immediately realized the idiocy of the question.

"What? Here?" The woman gave a bray of mirthless

laughter. "You must be joking! Look, dear, I'm sorry if he's let you down but I can't help you and that's all there is to it."

Losing interest, she returned to her paper and after a moment I turned and left her, bumping into another couple in the doorway as I went out.

Back in the car I went on driving for a while in the same direction, trying to itemize what new information I'd gleaned. There was very little of it but suddenly another picture clicked into focus in my mind, one that I had seen without registering as I made my discomfited exit from the hotel. That blue car which had been parked some way behind my own—surely I'd seen it before? And almost simultaneously came the certainty that it belonged to Marcus Sinclair.

I jammed my foot down on the brake, made a wide U-turn and drove swiftly back, but the road alongside the Picardy was now deserted. If I had recognized his car, I could be more or less sure that he had recognized mine, and therefore me, despite my attempt at disguise. But what had brought him to this unlikely neighbourhood I could not imagine, unless his low, cultured voice had been the one I'd first heard over the telephone. I had been too disturbed myself to notice his reaction to the mention of the Picardy that morning, but overall the only logical explanation for his presence there was that he had followed me. I felt a little tremor of alarm. Perhaps Sarah was not so wide of the mark in her assessment of him after all.

For the rest of the drive home I kept a lookout for the blue Triumph but there was no sign of it, nor was Marcus's car parked outside the Beeches when I reached it.

I made myself a cup of tea and sat down with it at the

kitchen table to assess the position. No doubt my telephone caller had been the "friend" who had left with Room 127 and later returned for his case. But who was the young lady who was anxiously making enquiries last Friday? Not, presumably, the one who should have received my message, because she would have known what had happened to him. There must therefore be two girls and a man connected with the disappearance—if there really had been a disappearance. It was all so bafflingly vague that I seemed to have come to a dead end in the puzzle I had set myself to solve. There was certainly nothing further to be gained by another visit to the Picardy, and as for the tenuous link with the theatre, it could of course have been sheer coincidence that Stephen had been whistling "Roses of Picardy." The only other possible line to pursue was to go back to square one, the place where it had all started—the estate agents' office.

I laid my cup carefully down on the saucer, aware of quickening excitement. They were short-staffed, obviously, or the office would not have been deserted when I called. And, as I had told Sarah, I needed to find a job. Teaching was obviously not open to me at the moment, but I had learned shorthand and typing one year when Carl's private secretary went down with glandular fever and was away for several months.

I went quickly into the hall and selected the local Yellow Pages directory from the table under the round window. There were two secretarial bureaus in Westhampton. Surely I could inveigle one of them into offering me a job at Culpepper's.

Chapter 5

THE woman across the desk smiled brightly. "And what kind of secretarial work do you feel would interest you, Miss Durrell?"

"Actually," I said firmly, "I'd rather like to work for an estate agent, if there are any jobs available in that line."

"Estate agents. I'll just check." She lifted a small card index file onto the desk and started to flick through it. "Of course all summer we've been desperately short of temps, but now that the holiday season is coming to an end there's not quite such a large choice on offer. However, I believe we have one or two which might interest you. Freeman and Lethbridge on the High Street are looking for—oh no, it's a junior they want. And—yes, Culpepper, Simpson and Clark, just a little bit further up the Parade here, are wanting someone for the next three weeks."

I let out my held breath. "That sounds ideal."

"Just a moment and I'll phone them to make sure they're not fixed up. People aren't always very reliable about letting us know when they find someone." She was dialling with her pencil as she spoke. It was clear almost at once that Culpepper's had not yet filled the vacancy and an appointment was made for me to go round straight away.

"You'll see Miss Davidson and Mr. Holding, Miss Durrell. I do hope the job's to your liking."

"Thank you." I stood up and added awkwardly, "Do I owe you anything if I accept?"

"No, no, it's the employer who sees to that. Good luck."

The walnut partitions shone as richly as they had done last Thursday. One telephone was still on the highly polished counter alongside the list of properties for sale. But this time the woman I'd seen through the window before was seated at a desk, and she rose quickly and came towards me.

"Miss Durrell? I'm Isobel Davidson. I wonder if you could give me a few particulars before I take you in to Mr. Holding?"

"Of course." I sat down opposite her and tried to gloss over the fact that although my shorthand and typing had reached good average speeds, I had never actually worked in an office. She prompted me at intervals, making notes in a small, neat hand, and I studied her while she did so, wondering again if she was the intended recipient for the message. She was about thirty-five or six, I guessed, unmarried, and with fair hair scraped severely back into a French pleat. She was tall, slim, smartly dressed and, to judge by the glasses perched on her nose, rather short-sighted. However hard I tried, I could not imagine her within the dubious confines of the Picardy Hotel.

I glanced across at an empty desk on which stood a covered typewriter. "Is the other girl still on holiday?" I asked casually.

"No, unfortunately she had a slight accident last week and since she had a week's holiday in hand it seemed sensible to take it now. I'm due to go myself on Saturday, but it looks doubtful now whether I shall be able to get away. Obviously you couldn't be left on your own so soon; it all depends on if Miss Derbyshire is well enough to come back on Monday. I'll take you now to see Mr. Holding—Mr. Alan Holding, that is. His son, Mr. Peter, is also a partner."

"What happened to Messrs. Culpepper, Simpson and Clark?"

She smiled. "Messrs. Culpepper and Clark are long since departed this life. Mr. Ernest Simpson is the senior partner, but he's semi-retired and only comes in occasionally."

She tapped on the glass door in the left-hand partition and showed me into the office which lay beyond. Mr. Alan Holding rose to his feet, a rather short man in his fifties with a small moustache and boyishly rosy cheeks. "Miss Durrell? I believe you may be able to help us out? Capital, capital!"

Twenty minutes later I was seated at the desk opposite Miss Davidson, typing out property details. So far, so good. However, if I'd expected all to be mysteriously revealed during the first few hours I spent at Culpepper's, I was to be disappointed. A more ordinary firm would have been hard to find. Peter Holding appeared and called me into his office to take down a few letters. He was about my own age, with long hair and a penchant for purple suits.

"Do you drive, Miss Durrell? Fine, then you wouldn't object to showing clients over properties where necessary?

Great. You'd better come with me once or twice first though, to learn the ropes."

The morning passed. At lunchtime, rather than drive back all the way to the Beeches, I merely crossed the Avenue and found a pleasant cake shop with a small restaurant above. I went up, seated myself at a window table, and stared down at the crowds of shoppers milling below. Beyond the pavement was the wide road, the gardens, and, discernible behind the fountain, the glass frontage of Culpepper's itself. And as my eyes located it, the door opened and Marcus Sinclair came quickly out and strode away up the road. Could I go *nowhere* without running across Marcus Sinclair? I wondered a little uneasily what business he had with Culpepper's and whether it could possibly have any bearing on the fact that I had started working there that very morning.

During the afternoon some clients called and later Peter Holding and I went with them to look round an empty house. By the end of that week I seemed to have been at the office for months but there had been no cryptic phone messages for me to intercept and no suspicious characters lurking round corners. Hating every moment of it, I had steeled myself to a quick flick through desks and filing cabinets as chance offered, but nothing untoward came to light, which fact made me feel guiltier than ever. Each lunchtime I returned to the same café and usually to the same table and it was there, on the Friday, that Marcus Sinclair found me.

"Mind if I join you?"

I turned quickly from the window in time to see him pulling out the chair beside me. "I saw you from the street. How are things?"

"All right, thank you."

"Managing to pass the time?"

"As a matter of fact," I said, my eyes fixed on him with a hint of challenge, "I've taken a job."

"Oh?" He was studying the menu.

"With Culpepper's, across the road."

"Good for you." If he was already aware of the fact, he was not going to admit it.

"You know the firm?" I prompted.

"Oh yes, they're pretty sound, I imagine. Long-established and all that. Unlikely to fold during your temporary employment, anyway!"

"I didn't mention that it was temporary."

His eyes met mine with some amusement. "But since you've only taken the flat for six months, it can hardly be permanent, can it?" He turned away to give his order to the waitress and I started to eat my meal. "You know something, *Miss Durrell?*" he went on deliberately, turning back to me, "I have a feeling that you're not quite what you seem to be."

I stared at him wordlessly while he unhurriedly leaned over and ran one finger over the white band on my ringless hand. I jerked back. "I don't know what you're talking about."

"For instance," he continued softly, "I would hazard a guess that you are in fact Mrs. Carl Clements."

I ran my tongue round dry lips and when I spoke at last my voice was shriller than I cared for. "What are you, an enquiry agent or something?"

He smiled. "Nothing so dramatic. Don't look so worried, it's no concern of mine. I won't give you away."

"But how—?"

"I recognized you back at the hotel. It was a chance in a thousand, I know, but I'd seen a photograph of you with your husband in an old magazine at the dentist's, only the week before. I am right, aren't I?"

I nodded. There was no point in denying it.

"I presume you've left him?"

Another nod.

"Permanently?"

"I don't know."

"Does he know where you are?"

"No." My breathing was rapid and shallow and I kept my eyes on my plate.

After a moment he said gently, "Isn't that rather cruel?" I did not reply. "You see, I know what he's going through. My wife left me, too. We're divorced now." He answered the unspoken query that must have been in my eyes. "Yes, I suppose I did deserve it, but that didn't make it hurt any the less at the time."

"Have you any children?"

"No. All nice and tidy." His voice was bitter. He leaned back while the waitress placed a bowl of soup in front of him and then, with a shrewd glance at my face, he said, "Anyway, enough of that. What really intrigues me is why you so obviously regard me with such dark suspicion. Am I indebted to the imaginative Mrs. Foss again?"

I crumbled the bread on my plate. His interest in me at the hotel was now doubly explained. He had recognized me and he'd heard me say I was going to live at his own address. His being at the window that night had also had a simple enough

64

explanation, as I'd really suspected all along. Which left—

"Did you follow me last Sunday afternoon?" I asked abruptly.

He met my eyes. "Yes, but I didn't think you'd noticed. I must be slipping!"

That, at least, was truthful. "May I ask why?"

"Because, though I couldn't imagine why, I was pretty sure you'd make a beeline for that grotty hotel and I didn't feel it was a safe place for you to go."

"You're trying to say you went along to keep an eye on me?"

"Exactly that."

"And you'd have stormed the barricades if I hadn't returned in reasonable time? That could have been embarrassing!"

"Don't be ridiculous, Ginnie." It was the first time he'd used my first name and he spoke impatiently. I flushed, resenting the reprimand although unwillingly aware that my facetiousness had warranted it.

"Are you going to tell me why you went?"

"No. I'm sorry."

"Something to do with your husband?"

My flush deepened. "Good Lord no!"

"Thank God for that, anyway. It was something those pansies said, wasn't it? You leaped as though you'd been stung when you heard the name of the place, so it must have rung some kind of a bell."

I stirred uneasily. "Marcus, what is your job? What do you do?"

"Changing the subject? All right. Well, I'm sorry to disappoint you, but there's nothing mysterious about it. I'm a building consultant. I draw plans for extensions, new houses, all that kind of thing, and see them through from the drawing board to the planning department and beyond. Satisfied?"

"Which is why you went to Culpepper's?"

"Of course, and Freeman's, and Jones, Henry. Why? Had that appeared sinister in some way too?"

"You work from home?"

"I do. It's easier and cheaper than paying for office premises. Next question!"

I smiled reluctantly. "I'm sorry. I have been a bit jumpy lately."

"I've noticed. But you're not going to tell me why?"

"Not at the moment, anyway. Heavens, look at the time! I must go."

I met Sarah that evening as I was walking back from garaging the car.

"What did you think of M.M.?" she demanded. "I bet he only came because of you. He'd seen you before somewhere, hadn't he? He seemed pretty attentive—you'd better watch him!"

I laughed. "Relax, Sarah, he's not in the microfilm business after all!" Briefly I told her of his joining me for lunch and the explanation of his job. She looked rather disappointed.

"Well, he certainly seems interested in you, whatever he does. How's your job going?"

"Okay. Having just got used to Miss Davidson, she's off on a fortnight's holiday today and on Monday I have to start getting to know the other girl." Who, I added privately,

66

might well be a likelier bet for my purposes than Isobel Davidson had proved.

Looking back on that week, it is obvious that I was treating the whole rigmarole as a sort of game, a mental stimulant in the same vein as a crossword puzzle. As time passed without any further development and the seeming mysteries surrounding Marcus were peeled innocently away, the initial uneasiness I had felt faded and I was far from convinced that anything untoward had actually taken place.

"How about you and Andy coming round for supper tomorrow evening?" I suggested impulsively. The weekend stretched emptily ahead and I wanted to avoid at all costs the danger of allowing myself time to brood over Carl.

"That would be super! I'd like him to see how the other half lives!"

It passed through my mind that Marcus would have made up a foursome, but I dismissed the idea at once. He wasn't much given to small talk, I didn't feel that he and the Fosses would find very much in common, and, most important to my way of thinking, it seemed wise not to become too involved with Marcus myself.

The following morning I met Kitty at the supermarket. "Have you been along to the theatre this week?" she asked, as we trundled our baskets side by side.

"No, have you?"

"A couple of times. Actually, I volunteered to go along and cook them some lunch tomorrow. They're rehearsing like mad all day and Laurence doesn't like going out for lunch—it breaks the continuity, he says. They've been living on sandwiches all week so I thought I'd rustle up something on the little stove at the theatre—nothing complicated, just a change from sandwiches."

Sunday was completely clear, a potential Carl-trap. "Like any help?"

"I certainly would!"

"What lines are you thinking along?"

"Oh, spaghetti Bolognese or something. I've bought a few tins of mince as a start."

"How many will be there?"

"About a dozen or so, I imagine, plus the stage manager, stage director and possibly some of the lighting people. I don't know how far they've got."

"What play are they doing?"

"*Twelfth Night.* They double up some of the minor parts, though."

"Suzanne Grey isn't in this one, is she?"

She glanced at me quickly. "No, which should make life easier."

"Is she temperamental?"

"Well, you presumably heard her at the party."

We joined the queue at the cash desk. "If you come along about eleven-thirty," Kitty said, "that will give us plenty of time and we can stay on and watch for a while if we feel like it."

It was a pleasant evening with the Fosses. Sarah as usual chattered incessantly and several times I caught her husband's amused eyes on her. He was a few years older than she, quiet and studious-looking with his dark-rimmed glasses. I gathered he was a junior partner in a firm of accountants over the other side of Westhampton.

"You realize," I remarked during the meal, "that I have been in the flat for one whole week?"

"Pamela and Stephanie will be arriving back sometime this weekend," Sarah said. "I hope they won't crash around too much overhead! I'm sure we must make a dreadful row, but Moira never complains. I suppose she's used to noise, living with the boys."

"I won't mind a bit of noise; it'll stop me feeling lonely," I replied, and then regretted the admission tacit in the remark.

"Do you get lonely, Ginnie? You seem very self-sufficient to me! I'm sure I couldn't bear to live alone."

"I'm sure you couldn't, darling," Andrew agreed with a laugh. "If you'd no one to talk to, you'd wilt away!"

"Not only that, I'd be scared stiff, specially sleeping on the ground floor."

"Don't be silly, Sarah!" Andrew's voice sharpened as he threw me an anxious glance.

"It's all right, Andy, Ginnie's not going to be put off by my prattling. I know it's silly, but the fact remains if I slept downstairs, I'd stay awake all night listening for footsteps!"

"You've made me feel a lot better!" I commented ruefully. "I'd never given it a thought before."

"I *told* you to shut up," Andrew said accusingly.

I smiled. "I was only joking. More coffee, Sarah?"

But that night after they had gone I made sure that all the windows except the bedroom ones were firmly closed, and even so I lay awake longer than usual listening to the wind in the trees just outside.

At eleven-thirty the following morning I parked the car in

the usual position and swung through the quiet streets to the Little Theatre. It was a dull day with a cool breeze which lifted my hair as I walked and made me glad I had decided to wear a trouser suit rather than a summer dress. I ran up the steep stairs with my shopping bag and turned into the kitchenette, where Kitty was unloading her own contributions onto the table.

"I bought some mushrooms and tomatoes to liven up the tinned mince," I said. "Also a green pepper I had left over from last night."

"Gorgeous, and I've brought some French loaves. We should have quite a feast. Remind me to pay you back for what you bought out of the petty cash. Is this pan big enough for the spaghetti, do you think?"

"Barely. We'd better do it in two batches." I hung my jacket on the back of the door and pushed up the sleeves of my sweater.

"We're getting a bit low on coffee," Kitty remarked, peering into the huge tin. "They must have been living on it this week. There's only just enough left for today."

"I could drop some in after work tomorrow if you like. It's no bother when I have the car."

"Thanks, that would be a great help. I'd certainly have trouble fitting it on my handlebars!"

Lunch was very informal, with some people sitting on the chairs round the walls of the foyer and the rest on the floor. Talk was mainly of the play and I drank it in avidly though I was perfectly content in my role of onlooker until Stephen, with a malicious gleam in his eye, drew me into the conversation.

"Well, Ginnie, aren't you going to give us the benefit of your opinion? I'm sure you'd be able to put us right!" Since the problem they were discussing had arisen once at the Playhouse, I was able to reply lucidly and even to suggest an improvement on the method they had chosen. Stephen was obviously taken aback at my unexpected competence. "Of course," he went on quickly, after Laurence Grey had thanked me warmly for the suggestion, "if you're not careful you can get bogged down with too many contrived effects, which eventually detracts from the drama rather than otherwise."

I smiled. "You mean 'Art for art's sake,' or *l'art pour l'art,* as Madame Lefevre always says."

My laughing words dropped into an icy pool of sudden silence. For at least ten seconds—and it seemed three times as long—no one even moved. Then Laurence Grey said a little breathlessly, *"Who* did you say?"

I swallowed nervously, aware of the gimlet concentration of every pair of eyes in the room but completely at a loss to understand why I had merited it. "Madame Lefevre. She's a wealthy French widow I know in London who takes a great interest in the theatre."

Laurence said smoothly, "I knew a Juliette Lefevre in Paris some years ago. I wonder if that could be any relation?" He was in control again now.

"I don't think so, no. She only had one son and he was killed in a road accident a few months ago."

"I see." Laurence's eyes were on me, considering, almost calculating. After a moment a perfunctory smile touched his mouth briefly and he looked away. I found that my neck was stiff, as though I had subconsciously held it in an immobility matching that of my companions. Carefully, with unsteady hands, I put my plate down on the floor and at the movement eyes dropped away from me and I was no longer under such intense scrutiny. I drew a quivering breath of relief.

Later, as Kitty and I washed the dishes side by side, I said with an attempt at casualness, "That was an odd reaction, about Madame Lefevre. Do you know what it was all about?"

"Search me. Perhaps Laurence had an affair with La Belle Juliette and was afraid of Papa with a shotgun in pursuit!"

"But it wasn't only Laurence that reacted."

"Sorry, Ginnie, it was lost on me." There was obviously no help forthcoming from Kitty. After we'd cleared away, we crept through to the auditorium and settled down in the back row to watch the progress of the rehearsal. On Carl's behalf I was particularly interested in Robert Harling's portrayal of Antonio and felt it came over very well. A girl I hadn't seen before, Joanna Lacy, made a very appealing Viola while Marion Dobie, whom I'd last seen as the mother in the Priestley play, was a rather elderly Olivia.

After a while Kitty glanced at her watch. "I'll have to go," she said regretfully. "It's Mum's birthday and I promised I'd be there for tea. Are you sure it won't be a nuisance having to collect the coffee tomorrow? One of the cast could always slip out."

"No, not at all. I'll drop it off on my way home."

"Right, thanks. Keep the receipt for reimbursement. Are you going to stay a bit longer?"

"I'll wait till the end of this scene, anyway."

72

She slipped away and I settled back as I'd done countless times in the past to watch movement and speech begin to coagulate, this time under the direction of Laurence Grey, slouched in the second row. "Can we have Malvolio on again please; this letter scene isn't gelling yet. Give Malvolio his cue, Liz: 'Here comes the trout that must be caught with tickling.' Okay, let's go."

I watched them go through it three or four times before he allowed them to pass on to the next scene, and by that time I was tired of sitting still. I left my seat quietly and pushed my way through the swing doors into the foyer. It was deserted—a coat slung over the bar, a cup and saucer pushed under one chair. I picked up the latter, carried them through to the kitchenette and retrieved my jacket and the empty shopping bag. No one was about, everyone being grouped on or around the stage engrossed in the rehearsal. I turned towards the stairs and then on an impulse, passed them and moved instead to the bend in the passage beyond. It was a fascinating old building, this, with countless hidden nooks and crannies and now seemed as good a time as any to explore it. A long corridor, dim and unlit, stretched away ahead of me to another bend where it turned once more to the right, presumably in the direction of the stage. The left-hand wall was bare along its entire length but there were two or three doors on the right. I started silently along the passage, wondering rather nervously if I was trespassing. I turned the knob of the first door but it would not yield. The next one was more forthcoming and opened onto a dusty storeroom, full of stacked chairs and trestle tables. The third room was empty except for an old washbasin leaning drunkenly on the

73

floor. By this time I had come to the bend. The corridor continued beyond it but a few yards further on a short flight of steps led upwards, presumably to the wings, but a door at the top blocked off what lay behind. The passage itself continued beyond the stairs and after a moment's hesitation, so did I. Somewhere in the distance now I could see light and the faint noise of voices from the stage reached me.

Suddenly I stiffened. No, the voices weren't coming from the stage; they were nearer at hand. Someone was coming. Instinct told me I should not be discovered here and I glanced quickly over my shoulder. There was not time to reach the bend in the passage; the voices were growing louder. I turned and fled silently back to the stairs, swung myself round the post and up the steps two at a time. The door at the top resisted my frantic fingers. It was securely locked. I was trapped. Crouching down, I pressed myself into the bannister as closely as I could, hoping desperately that whoever was coming would not glance back as they passed the stairs. My heart seemed literally to be in my mouth, great muffled beats which were painful to swallow past. Footsteps came nearer and I heard Stephen's voice quite clearly. "Suppose he goes on refusing to eat?"

"God knows. You tell me." It was a girl's voice, offhand and sullen. And then they were there, scarcely six feet below me. I tucked my head down behind the cumbersome bag I was still carrying and pressed still further back in my corner, not daring to look down in case the force of my gaze should communicate itself to them. And a moment later, blessedly, they turned the corner of the passage and their footsteps faded away. Time passed and at last, stiff and cold from my cramped position, I pulled myself to my feet and, as though suddenly released from paralysis, fled down the passages and the steep stairs and out into the mews. Minutes later, my heart still beating a tattoo high in my chest, I was in the car and driving like a maniac for home. Only then, in the safety of familiar surroundings, did I stop to wonder why I had panicked so. Technically I might have been trespassing, but I had never heard that the passage beyond the staircase was private property. I could have stood my ground and explained to whoever was coming that I had been exploring and hoped it was all right. But the fact that it had been Stephen who came only reinforced my thankfulness that I had not been seen, for if after all there was some undercurrent at the theatre, Stephen Darby was undoubtedly behind it.

Chapter 6

THROUGHOUT Sunday evening my mind kept going back to the two new puzzles which the afternoon at the theatre had presented: the curious reaction by practically everyone present to my casual mention of Madame Lefevre and the tantalizingly brief fragment of conversation I had overheard in the dark passageway.

I also spent some time wondering who the girl with Stephen could have been. Liz, Joanna and Marion were on or around the stage, Kitty had presumably gone home long since, Suzanne Grey had not been at the theatre at all. The only other girl at lunch had been June Seacombe the stage director and she must surely have been fully occupied with the rehearsal. The one positive thing in the whole affair was that Stephen had once more had a part to play in the mystery. I told myself that the remark could have been passed about a dog or cat which was off its food, but one explanation which I hardly dared acknowledge was surely that the he who was not eating was the man who had never known what hit him and had left the Picardy Hotel trustingly with his "friend" only to disappear into thin air.

I was still occupied with these theories the next morning when I drove once more to Culpepper's. Miss Derbyshire was there before me, her left wrist in a bandage. She was small and dark with rather a sulky face overshadowed by exceptionally heavy and unplucked eyebrows.

"I'm not going to be much use to you," she greeted me unenthusiastically. "I can't even drive yet, so you'll have to cope with all the client-cosseting as well as the typing. I'll do the bookkeeping, though, and anything that can be copied by hand."

"I believe you had an accident? What happened?"

"It was too stupid. I slipped and fell for no reason on my way to work one morning. Someone very kindly whipped me straight off to the Out Patients to have my wrist x-rayed. I was lucky it wasn't broken; it was bent right back under me. Anyway, there were only two days of the week left and I was due to be off all last week, so I simply went home. How have things been here?"

"Pretty quiet, really."

"Has 16 Crofton Road gone yet?"

"Not that I know of."

"I said all along they'd have to bring the price down." She leaned back in her chair and watched me set out papers on the desk. "So old Isobel's gone away—I never thought she would."

"Oh?"

She smiled spitefully. "Didn't you notice? She and His Lordship"—she jerked her head in the direction of Mr. Holding's office—"they've got a very cosy little arrangement going."

"Really?" I felt uncomfortable but at a loss to know how to halt her unwelcome confidences.

"Yes, his wife's an invalid so it's all very convenient. They've been having it off for years. You wouldn't think so to look at her, would you? Prim and prissie and butter-wouldn't-melt." She gave a short, derisive laugh and I reflected ruefully that it hadn't taken me long to decide that I did not like Miss Derbyshire.

For once I actually hoped that Marcus would join me for lunch again but he did not come. I would have welcomed the chance to talk to someone reasonably pleasant for a change. When I had finished my meal I walked along to a grocer's to buy the coffee I had promised to take to the theatre. It was spitting with rain as I returned to the office and I felt unaccountably depressed. At least I was spared any further conversation with the surly Miss Derbyshire; Peter Holding collected me almost as soon as I got back and whipped me off to pick up some clients and escort them round a flat. It was five o'clock by the time we returned to the office and Miss Derbyshire had already gone home. I breathed a sigh of relief. I was not looking forward to the next two weeks in her company.

The rain had settled in now and as I hurried from the car through to Phoenix Street it was coming down quite heavily, darkening the shoulders of my jacket and stinging my cheeks with its sharp cold needles. Clutching the tin of coffee, I ran lightly up the stairs and into the foyer, straight into an unexpected crowd of people who were gathered round a tall, fair man with his back to me. Laurence saw my hesitant approach and smiled.

"Ah, the angel of mercy with the coffee!"

The stranger turned, and all the breath was driven out of my body with the force of a sledge hammer.

"Ginnie!" The word seemed to be jolted out of him. "What in hell are you doing here?"

I said aridly, "Hello, Carl."

From behind me Stephen's voice came incongruously. "Ah, Ginnie, I thought I heard you. Let me introduce you to someone whom you can boast about to those theatrical friends of yours."

"I rather think, Steve," Laurence Grey broke in drily, "that introductions are unnecessary. It would seem that Mr. Clements and Miss Durrell have already met."

"Miss Durrell?" Carl's voice was wrongly pitched and the look on his face dissipated any pleasure I might have felt at Stephen's obvious discomfiture. "Yes indeed," he went on after a moment, "Miss Durrell and I are old acquaintances —one might almost say sparring partners."

I wrenched my eyes away from his. "Well, I won't hold you up any longer. I'll just leave the coffee in the kitchen."

Stephen said evenly, "Don't run away, Ginnie. Stay and join the party."

"No, really, I must go."

"Then I'll see you home." Carl's voice did not invite argument but I said feebly, "Really, it's all right—I have the car."

He had taken my arm. "I'll be back later," he said over his shoulder, and marched me out of the foyer and down the stairs, leaving them all staring after us. Out in the mews

79

puddles lay between the cobblestones and the rain slanted down. Carl said in a low voice, "God, Ginnie, if you knew the state I've been in. Why did you do it? Why ever didn't you let me try to explain?"

"Explain?" I choked over the word. "From what I saw, no explanation was necessary. I couldn't take any more, Carl; it's as simple as that."

We had paused on the roadway and now he turned his collar up with his free hand and looked up and down the street. "Where's the car, for Pete's sake?"

"Through the alleyway. Carl, please don't come with me."

"We have to talk, Ginnie. I'm not going to let you vanish out of sight again. These last two weeks have been pretty grim, I can tell you."

"I haven't exactly enjoyed them myself."

"But you don't seem to have wasted any time in making a new life for yourself," he said bitterly. He stopped again and looked down at me, the rain plastering his hair against his forehead. "How did you get mixed up with that theatre crowd, anyway?"

"It's the story of my life, isn't it? I never learn."

He still hesitated but I started to walk again and he fell into step beside me. At last, drenched and uncomfortable, we reached the car. "Please let me go, Carl. I'm not in any state to go over everything just now."

"Give me the key."

He took it out of my hand and opened the door. "You'd better drive. I don't know my way round this godforsaken place." Ridiculous that everything hinged on the rain. If he hadn't looked so wet and bedraggled I would probably have driven off without him. As it was, I hesitated and was lost.

"Where's your own car?"

"Being serviced. This all blew up unexpectedly, so I had to come by train."

The drive home was a nightmare, the gleaming, prematurely darkened streets, the wet clothes sticking to my body and the tense, silent figure of Carl beside me.

"Where are you going?" His voice sharpened as I came round the third corner of the square and drew up outside the Beeches.

"Home—my flat." I was beginning to shake now, a mixture of trembling and shivering.

"Your *flat?*" His voice was incredulous. "You mean you're not at a hotel?"

"I can't stay at a hotel indefinitely," I said through juddering lips.

"Indefinitely?"

Something snapped inside me. I said shrilly, "Do you have to repeat everything I say?"

"Ginnie—" He broke off and I saw him moisten his lips. "Look, this has gone far enough." He moved impatiently. "Hell, let's go inside where we can at least talk in comfort."

"No, Carl." My hands were laced tightly together.

"What do you mean, no?"

"I don't want you to come in. I told you, there's nothing to say."

"There's one hell of a lot to say!" he said explosively. "How you can just—my God, have you any idea of the *embarrassment* you've caused me, quite apart from anything else? How do you think I felt, ringing round all our friends

81

and saying, 'Please, is Ginnie there?' And all the time—"

"It must have been most humiliating," I said stiffly. "I'm sorry your pride was hurt, but I doubt if anything else was."

He said furiously, "What do I have to do to make you see—"

I had had more than enough. I tore the car door open and half fell outside. In the same moment Carl flung himself out the other side and in two strides had caught hold of my arm again, swinging me round to face him.

"Let me go!" I cried wildly.

"Ginnie, will you for God's sake be reasonable!"

Beside us Marcus's voice said calmly, "Can I be of any help?"

Carl released me so suddenly that I stumbled and Marcus's arm came round to steady me. For a second longer Carl stood there, magnificent in the rain, staring down at us. Then without a word he turned on his heel and strode off.

"He hasn't got a car," I said foolishly through trembling lips.

"I'm worried!" Marcus retorted grimly. "Give me your key, there's a good girl. I've never been particularly in favour of pneumonia."

I thrust my handbag at him and a moment later we were inside the little hall, dripping on the emerald carpet.

"Have you any drink in the house?"

I shook my head. We'd had wine on Saturday evening but it had all been finished and I'd never cared for spirits.

"Then go and get out of those wet things while I put the kettle on."

"Marcus, it was—"

"I know who it was. Do as I say, Ginnie."

I didn't seem able to stop shaking, but I went through to the bedroom and hung my soaking wet trouser suit over the radiator. It didn't occur to me until I went to bed that night that the heating wasn't turned on. I rubbed ineffectually at my hair and went back to the kitchen, where Marcus was pouring boiling water into the teapot. He took one look at my face, put the lid quickly on the pot and came towards me.

"I'm all right," I said quickly. He hesitated and then went back to the teapot. "Sit down then and I'll pour." After a moment he added, "I can't say I care for your husband's manners."

"He wasn't at his best. Marcus, he looked so strained." I took a quick sip of the strong tea.

"It's hardly surprising. He probably feels strained, too. How did he find out where you were?"

"He didn't. I just ran into him at the theatre."

"Where?"

"The Little Theatre. I've been helping out a bit by serving coffee and so on. Carl must have come down to see one of the actors. When I appeared, he was as shattered as I was."

"I can imagine." Outside the window a skein of rain hung heavily across the garden, blotting out the last of the daylight several hours too soon. I pictured Carl walking about the streets not knowing where he was.

"Would you like me to stay for a bit?"

I pulled my attention back to Marcus. "No, thank you. I'm all right. Thanks very much for your support."

"Well, you know where I am if you want me." He let himself out and I sat for a long time at the kitchen table while

83

the dregs in the teacups grew cold and the rain darkened steadily outside. Eventually I went through to the drawing room. I didn't put the light on. The park opposite was huddled under the dripping umbrella of its trees. I sat down in one of the easy chairs and all my surmises about Stephen and the theatre and Culpepper's and the Picardy gave way to pulsating, agonizing thoughts of Carl. The phone rang and I went through the dark hall and lifted it. His voice said, "Don't hang up, Ginnie."

I said dully, "How did you find the number?"

"Grey got it from some girl." Of course, I'd given it to Kitty. "Ginnie, may I come round, please?"

I shook my head, remembered he couldn't see me, and said, "No."

"But we have to talk. How can I get through to you if—"

"I don't want to see you."

His voice changed. "Is that fellow still there?"

"No," I said wearily.

"Look, Gin, I know I made things even worse this afternoon. Seeing you so unexpectedly completely threw me, and then finding out you were calling yourself Miss Durrell and had a flat of your own and a new circle of friends, and seem to have written me off completely— Ginnie, please come home."

"This is my home now."

There was a long silence. I wondered vaguely if he had hung up. Then he said, "I see. Just one more question, then, and I'll stop bothering you. Why did you decide to come to Westhampton?"

The complete change of direction bewildered me. After a

84

moment I said slowly, "I don't know. Does it matter?"

"It might do, yes."

"Well, I'm sorry but I've no idea why I came here. The coast road was blocked," I added lamely.

"Obviously something else you refuse to discuss." His voice was crisp. "And I suppose you can't tell me either how you managed in such a short time to become so involved in the Little Theatre?"

"Look," I protested weakly, "what is this? You know I was interested in the theatre long before I met you."

There was a pause and then he said briskly, "Sorry, Ginnie, I don't think that's quite good enough. A word of warning, though. I know more than you think."

I said helplessly, "Carl, I've no idea—"

"Goodbye, Ginnie." The phone clicked in my ear. Carefully I replaced it on the cradle. His last words had sounded incredibly like a threat. *Carl—?* Beyond the round hall window the wet branches of the beech trees lashed and writhed, invisible and somehow menacing. I reached up and wrenched the curtain across the glass. Then at last I snapped on the lights, in the hall and throughout the flat, running from one room to another as though the darkness were something tangible that must be kept at bay.

It was eight o'clock and I still hadn't eaten. I opened a tin of soup and drank it standing up in the kitchen. I felt bruised and battered and I was still subject to bouts of violent trembling. The phone sounded again. I let it ring for a while but eventually, as on that fateful occasion at Culpepper's, I had to answer it.

Marcus said anxiously, "Are you all right, Ginnie?"

85

"I'm all right," I said.

"I looked out a few minutes ago and the flat seemed to be in darkness. Try not to worry. He can't force you to go back."

"No."

"Would you like to come up here and have a drink with me?"

"No, thank you. I think I'll just have a hot bath and go to bed with a couple of aspirins."

"Have you had anything to eat?"

"Some soup, yes."

"All right. Sleep well."

"Thanks for phoning."

Carl was probably in the train back to London by now. I pictured him taking a taxi and letting himself into the empty flat. Had anyone thrown the dead roses away? Strange how my mind kept harking back to them. They were a symbol of the unreal existence we had had together—champagne and roses. And now the roses would be dead, curled up, withered, dry. I thought—I could have gone back with him tonight. He wanted me to. I could have forgotten about the Beeches and the job and all the needling question marks that had surrounded me in Westhampton. For a time at least he would have been careful not to upset me again. We would have resumed the phrenetic round of drinks and parties and first nights and beautiful women whose eyes frankly wondered whatever Carl had seen in a mouse like me.

My teeth fastened in my lip. This evening had left me in no doubt of my feelings for him but it was all so useless, so completely hopeless. My mind shied blisteringly away from the quicksands of what might have been and skidded to a halt in another direction. Whatever had he meant by those last two questions? Had I had my wits about me, I could have retaliated with one of my own: why had he himself come today? "It blew up unexpectedly," he'd said. What had? I'd assumed he had come to see Robert Harling but the play wasn't on this week. A little tremor of apprehension crawled over my scalp.

"I know more than you think," he had said. Could Carl possibly be connected in some way with all those labyrinthine threads—the Picardy, the man in Room 127? Was it Stephen rather than Robert he had come to see? "A word of warning," he had said.

With a numb feeling of disbelief I went round the flat once more, this time to switch off the lights. The hot bath soothed and comforted my body but it couldn't reach the whirling, clicking computer of my brain which had embarked on a wild, push-button marathon of conjecture. Carl knew Madame Lefevre better than I did. Had the theatre crowd heard of her through him? In any event, there was surely nothing sinister about her. And what possible harm did he imagine I could do, that he felt it necessary to "warn" me?

Shivering in the soft towel despite the steamy heat of the small room, I resolved bleakly to trust no one, not even Marcus. For if Carl of all people could suddenly emerge as a potential enemy, then the world was indeed upside-down.

Chapter 7

I WAS heavy-eyed and emotionally drained the next morning, but like an automaton I drove to Culpepper's. Miss Derbyshire looked at me across the covered mound of her typewriter. "I hear you've been deputizing for me in more ways than one."

I stared at her blankly. "I'm afraid I don't understand."

She seemed to be trying to gauge the truth of my reply. "At the theatre," she said at last, "helping Kitty."

A host of little alarm buzzers sounded in my head. "The girl who usually helps me has sprained her wrist." That was the only half-memory I had time to pinpoint.

"You're Rachel?"

"I am indeed."

I attempted a smile. "It's a small world."

"You didn't know?"

"Of course I didn't know. How should I?"

Her eyes were on me, unwinking black buttons. "My brother was most intrigued to learn you'd turned up here, too."

"Your brother?"

"Stephen. Stephen Darby." When I didn't, because I couldn't, speak, she added, "He dropped the 'shire' for the stage and changed the 'e' to 'a.' "

She had slipped on the way to work—that Thursday, obviously, and been taken straight to hospital, unable to contact him. This link between Culpepper's and the theatre was the one clue I needed to confirm my suspicion that it was Stephen who had phoned. No wonder he had been intrigued to learn I was here; he could surely be in no doubt now that it was I who had received his hurried message. Quite suddenly, it seemed that I had made a dangerous and criminally stupid mistake in coming to work here.

Back-pedalling desperately, I said with an attempt at lightness, "Well, now that you're back, I can at least relinquish my theatre duties to you."

"I doubt if you'll get away with that."

My eyes skidded to her face. "How do you mean?"

"From what I hear, you caused quite a stir there last night, sweeping off arm-in-arm with Carl Clements. They won't let you out of their clutches now that they know you have the ear of the great man."

I said numbly, "I haven't any influence with him."

"You'll never convince them of that. Believe me, you'll be surprised how popular you are the next time you go there."

"Well, I certainly won't be going as often now," I said a little wildly. "After all, I was only helping out in your absence."

"But I gathered you'd made yourself indispensable, advising them on production and Lord knows what else."

Obviously Stephen wouldn't readily forgive me for that.

To my untold relief, the bell rang in Mr. Holding's office and, with a final lingering look at me, Rachel picked up her notebook and went inside.

The palms of my hands were sticky with sweat. I took a handkerchief out of my bag and wiped them carefully, trying to anchor my whirling thoughts into some semblance of order. It now seemed obvious that Stephen was the "friend" who had come back to collect the luggage from Room 127, and also that it had been Rachel with him at the theatre on Sunday. "Suppose he goes on refusing to eat." So they must still have him hidden away somewhere, but who he was and why there had been no publicity about his disappearance I couldn't begin to guess. Briefly I wondered if I should make some kind of a statement to the police, but there was so little I could tell them. There was no shred of evidence to prove that anyone had disappeared at all, and only my own word that I'd intercepted the cryptic message that had started it all.

After her unwarranted burst of conversation, Rachel, to my relief, retreated into surly silence for the rest of the morning. At twelve-thirty I was preparing to go to lunch when Marcus came in. He nodded to Rachel and turned to me.

"Hello, Ginnie, how are things?"

"Fine, thank you." My eyes willed him not to make any unguarded comment.

"Are you coming across the road for lunch?"

"Not today, no, I've rather a lot of shopping to do. I'll have to settle for a sandwich in a snack bar today."

"According to the menu in the window they have steak and kidney pie on!"

I smiled. "The answer's still no, but I hope you enjoy it."

"Oh, well, I tried!" He went over and tapped on Mr. Holding's door and at his answer, went inside.

"Quite the little gadabout, aren't you?" Rachel remarked acidly. "A different man for each day of the week!"

"A slight exaggeration," I said lightly, picking up my bag. "I'll be back at one-thirty."

I hadn't any shopping, but I was in no state to face a tête-à-tête with Marcus. In my present weakened condition I might all too easily find myself confiding in him, which could be dangerous. Since I had effectively cheated myself out of a proper lunch, I went perforce to the snack bar round the corner, making the most of melamine table tops and plastic pepper pots, though as it happened the ruse was unnecessary, since he was still with Mr. Holding when I returned. Shortly afterwards they came out of the inner room together and as Mr. Holding stopped for a word with Rachel, Marcus leaned over my desk.

"How about dinner, since you couldn't make lunch?"

"I—can't tonight, I'm afraid."

"Can't, or won't?"

I flushed, but before I could think of a reply, Mr. Holding finished with Rachel and stood waiting at the door and Marcus joined him and went out without a backward glance.

One of the phone calls during the afternoon was, surprisingly, for me. Rachel had answered it, and a sarcastic smile spread over her face as she looked across at me. Without a word she handed me the receiver.

"Ginnie? Joanna Lacy here. I was wondering if Mr. Clements would like complementary tickets for the first night on Thursday week?"

"I really don't know," I said hesitantly, uncomfortably aware of Rachel's interest. "I think he might."

"Good. Then if you'll just let me have his address, I'll see that he gets a couple."

That was one trap I was not likely to fall into. "You can always reach him at the Playhouse Theatre."

"Oh, thanks. You'll be coming too, won't you?"

"I hope so."

"Will you be at the rehearsals again this week? I'd rather like to ask you about the interpretation of a few lines in Act Three."

Conscious of Rachel's grin, I said a little shortly, "I'm not a drama coach, Joanna, and I'm sure Laurence wouldn't like me butting in."

She laughed. "Oh, come on, don't be stuffy! It's only a very minor point, he probably wouldn't even notice, but it is open to two interpretations and I'm interested to know what you make of it. After all, you know the play backwards, don't you? Are you free this evening, by any chance?"

I knew resignedly that I would have to face them all sometime and probably the sooner it was over, the better— something to do with getting back on the horse after it had thrown you. And I had certainly been thrown last night. It would also back up my refusal of Marcus's dinner invitation.

"All right, I'll look in after work."

"I told you you wouldn't be allowed to stay away," Rachel said smugly as I put the phone down.

"Were you at the theatre on Sunday?" I asked suddenly, and had the satisfaction of seeing a guarded look come to her face.

"Only very briefly. Why?"

"You weren't there at lunchtime."

"No, I didn't get back from the parents' till after three. Those Sunday trains are the very devil."

That was probably true. If she had been there only briefly she would barely have had time to discuss essentials with Stephen, which explained why he hadn't mentioned me and my comment about Madame Lefevre, which had apparently made such an impression on them all. Certainly Rachel had not known yesterday of my connection with the theatre; just as certainly, she knew all the relevant details today.

Her cynicism had at least prepared me for the open arms which greeted me at the theatre, but the image of Carl was still blazoned on the foyer and my control was rocky, to say the least.

"Gosh, Ginnie, you should have seen their faces!" Liz Payne said with a laugh. "Talk about dumbfounded! Have you known him long?"

There seemed little point in persisting in my secrecy. "He's my husband," I said flatly.

Their reactions were simultaneous and I was deluged with their excited questions and exclamations. I said rapidly, "With all due respect, I didn't come here to discuss Carl Clements. Joanna, if you want me to go over that bit with you—"

"Yes, of course. Sorry, Ginnie. It's in the third act." She gave a warning shake of the head to the others, which i wasn't supposed to see, and with a tight throat I went with her into a corner and read through the scene, trying to

93

remember the interpretation Carl had put on it three years ago at the Playhouse.

When we had finished I said casually, "Why did he come here yesterday, anyway?"

"Who? Oh—I'm not sure. He spoke to Laurence for some time. Something to do with Robert, I gather. Lucky devil! I wish he'd take us all lock, stock and barrel! That would solve a lot of difficulties!"

"What difficulties?"

"Oh, money problems, you know the kind of thing."

"Is the theatre short of money?" I asked carefully.

"What theatre isn't? Well, all right, the Playhouse, presumably! But in the provinces it's always the same—rents go up, leases run out—"

Stephen came past and stopped on seeing me. "Well, well, Mrs. Clements!"

"Ginnie will do," I said steadily.

"You must have enjoyed yourself immensely, laughing up your sleeve at us all."

"Now look, Stephen," I began hotly, but he interrupted me.

"And I believe you're working at the same place as my sister, yet another coincidence."

"Yes, isn't it? I'd no idea who she was till she told me this morning. You don't look at all alike." He was, in fact, much more prepossessing than Rachel. He was leaning against the door jamb with arms folded, looking down at me.

"How long have you been there?"

I met his eyes calmly. "I started last Monday—just over

94

a week." It was a forlorn hope, but the fact that I wasn't officially there on the day of the phone call might give him pause.

"What made you decide to take that particular job?"

"My goodness, Steve!" I said lightly. "What an inquisition!"

His eyes fell. "I'm sorry, but you're full of surprises, Ginnie. You can't blame me for wondering how many others you might spring."

"My life," I said flippantly, getting to my feet, "is an open book! I took the job simply because they had a vacancy, it was something I could do, and I needed some cash. Okay?" Carl would have been proud of me, I thought sourly. "If that's all I can do, Joanna, I'll go now. There's a program I want to see on television."

"Thanks so much for coming. See you tomorrow?"

"I shouldn't think so."

"Try to drop in sometime, it's exciting when the play begins to fall into shape." She gave a self-conscious little laugh. "But of course, I don't have to tell you that!"

"I doubt if there's anything any of us can tell Mrs. Clements," said Stephen.

I met his eye. "I'll try not to put you in your place too often," I said sweetly, and heard Joanna's amused laugh. None of which, I reflected wryly on my way down the stairs, had endeared me any more to Stephen Darby. However, there was a limit to the amount I would take lying down, and he and his poisonous sister might as well realize that.

Since it was still early enough to be available for dinner with Marcus, I stopped at a steak house further along Phoenix Street and the blueness of evening was in the air by the time I emerged and drove home.

Two girls I hadn't seen before were coming out of the garage next to mine as I swung the door shut. The taller one came over. "Hello, you must be our new neighbour from Number Seven. I'm Stephanie Brigg."

"Ginnie Durrell. Did you have a good holiday?"

"Fabulous, thanks. This is my cousin, Pamela. I hear we missed one of Sarah's parties."

"Yes, it was very enjoyable."

"What did you think of our pretty boys?" Pamela asked with a twinkle.

"The photographers? Too gorgeous for words! I loved their pastel suits."

"Not to mention, of course, the carefully casual lock of hair!"

"Oh, Pam," Stephanie protested with a laugh.

"Well, you passed the acid test yourself, anyway," Pamela went on. "We met old Miss Cavendish this morning and she informed us you seemed a 'pleasant gel'!"

"That's reassuring!"

We had reached our front doors by this time and I left them to go up the stairs to their flat above mine. I was glad to have met them, unaccountably relieved that I wasn't alone stuck out in my little wing any longer. Sarah's words about the ground floor had stayed with me and to my suddenly apprehensive eyes everywhere looked very accessible.

I switched on the drawing-room lights and immediately the world outside deepened from blue to black. I went across to draw the curtains. It was still damp and raw after yester-

96

day's rain and the man on the seat in the park opposite could not have been very comfortable, though he obviously had excellent eyesight to be able to read his paper in that difficult light.

The television program I had given as my excuse to leave Joanna, scheduled for rather later than I had implied, was about to start. I made a quick round of the flat checking doors and windows, then I settled down for a pleasant hour or two of relaxation. From time to time I could hear the girls moving about in the flat above, and this added to my sense of well-being. I was tired, probably reaction from the emotional upheaval of the previous day, and I was in bed and asleep by soon after ten-thirty.

At first, I wasn't sure what had awakened me. I lay still, wrapped in the coils of the dream from which I had been roused, and then the sound came again. It was the doorbell. I sat up slowly, looking at the luminous face of the clock on the bedside table. It was one o'clock. What emergency could have made someone call at this hour? Panic explanations juggled for position in my mind. Tremblingly I slipped on my dressing gown and padded out into the hall. All was quiet.

I put my mouth against the solid wood of the door. "Who is it?"

There was no reply. I waited, a fluttering sensation at the base of my throat. There was no window in the flat that gave onto the stretch of gravel by the front door, and I had not the slightest intention of opening it until I knew who was there. For timeless minutes, measured only by my rapid heartbeats, I waited shiveringly in the hall. There was complete silence, not even the sound of retreating footsteps. At last, chilled and thoroughly frightened, I crept back to bed. Only when daylight began to seep into the room was I at last able to snatch a couple of hours' unbroken sleep before the alarm clock jangled me into full consciousness again.

It was with a slight sense of shock, when I drew back the curtains, that I noticed the man still seated on the park bench. For a moment I wondered if he were ill, even dead, before reason came to my aid. It was not the same man; this one was older and differently dressed. It seemed an odd whim that should have taken him to the park at eight o'clock on a late September morning, but he was breaking no law that I could see. It occurred to me for the first time that my own movements would be almost totally visible to anyone seated in that vantage point, since both drawing room and bedroom gave onto the park. It was not a pleasant thought, particularly in view of the night's adventure. I stood for a moment longer staring across, but the man was apparently deep in his paper and I eventually abandoned him and went through to the kitchen to make breakfast.

When I saw Stephanie and Pamela again at the garages, I asked casually, "Is the park opposite locked at night?"

"I couldn't say. I've never really thought about it. I dare say it should be, but the railings are so low that anyone who wanted to could easily climb over them. Why?"

"I just wondered," I answered vaguely.

The week wore on. I did not go to the theatre again and at the office Rachel was as unforthcoming as ever. I reflected that I only had one more week at Culpepper's, and was thankful. Rachel was on her guard with me now and there was nothing else to be learned there.

98

On the Friday evening Carl phoned. "Ginnie, I'm coming down to Westhampton for the first night on Thursday; they've sent me tickets. I shan't be able to get there much before the performance, but I'd be glad if you would arrange to meet me at the theatre and have dinner with me afterwards." His businesslike tone managed to convey that he expected my instant compliance.

"I'm not sure that I'll be free," I said on principle.

"Please arrange to be. There's no need to panic. It will be strictly business." And he rang off, leaving me seething at his high-handedness. This was a side of Carl that consistently irritated his associates but he had never shown it to me before. Obviously I had forfeited my right to any special privileges.

The next phone call was from Kitty. "Ginnie, you won't feel, will you, that we don't want you any more now that Rachel's back? I'd hate you to think we'd just been making use of you."

"And," I interrupted with a smile, "she can't do much anyway at the moment, with her wrist still bandaged."

"It's not that at all," Kitty said indignantly. She added with a giggle, "But I do have to confess I'd much rather have you with me. Will you be coming over the weekend?"

I hesitated. The long hours of Saturday and Sunday stretched barrenly ahead of me and I found I was not looking forward to spending them alone at the flat, with the possibility of unexplained doorbells and a motionless figure in the park across the way.

"Yes, Kitty, of course I'll come. Lunch again? I'll see you about eleven-thirty then."

The following morning I went out early to do the weekend shopping before going on to the theatre. As I swung the car out of the driveway and turned left to drive past the house, I was vaguely conscious of a flicker of movement at Marcus's window, but when I turned my head fully, no one was in sight. No doubt he was closing or opening the window again, I thought with a touch of self-mockery. I was becoming altogether too jumpy these days.

If the others were glad to see me at the theatre, very obviously Stephen and his sister were not. Stephen gave me a curt nod, Rachel not even that. Outwardly unperturbed, I joined Kitty in the kitchen and set to work on preparing chili con carne. As before, we ate it companionably grouped round the foyer. There was a noticeable change in the cast's attitude to me compared with last weekend. The glamour of Carl had rubbed off a little onto me. They brought me more often into the conversation and listened respectfully to my most banal replies. And all the time Stephen Darby sat with a mirthless twist to his mouth and his half-closed eyes on my face.

I watched the rehearsal after lunch and, as Joanna had predicted, felt the usual thrill of accomplishment as all the different passages began to fall neatly into place. I did notice, however, that the innovation which I had reluctantly discussed with Joanna on Tuesday had not after all been incorporated. However much he admired Carl, Laurence Grey was obviously not going to stand for interference with his own direction. I didn't blame him.

It was almost seven o'clock before he called a halt to the rehearsal and I was stiff with sitting so long in the seat at the

100

back of the stalls. I stood up and stretched. Marion Dobie called, " 'Bye, Ginnie; thanks for the lunch. See you tomorrow?"

"Probably," I said. I was glad to have the theatre to come to, despite Stephen and his sister, and the slight uneasiness I felt there. It was, after all, a second home to me. The lights in the foyer were out but the one at the stairhead gave enough reflected light to make it unnecessary to switch on the kitchen light as I went to collect my basket. The chili had made me thirsty, despite subsequent cups of tea, and I stopped to fill a cup with water at the sink and drank it slowly. I had rinsed and dried it and was almost back at the door when Stephen's voice just outside made me instinctively dart back out of sight. He was speaking quickly in a low voice, and from my position immediately behind the open door, I could hear quite clearly.

"I tell you I don't like it, Laurence. That girl's his wife and he's pally with the old dame. For all we know they've got a lead on us and he sent her ahead to spy out the land."

Rigid and unbreathing, I waited for Laurence's reply.

"Oh, I don't think so. He didn't know she was here. I'd stake my life on that. You should have seen his face when she walked in."

Stephen snorted. "He's an actor, isn't he? And added to that, she turns up at Culpepper's."

"What the hell has that got to do with it?"

There was a brief pause. So Stephen had not told Laurence of the phone call that went astray. "Well, she might be keeping an eye on Rachel," he said at last.

"Perhaps." Laurence Grey's voice was jerky with strain.

I heard the whir of his cigarette lighter and a spurt of flame through the door hinge enabled me to see his face for a moment, red-shadowed like a demon's. "I just wish to God we'd never started it. If I'd had any idea it would drag on this long—"

He broke off as a crowd of actors came together through the foyer and he and Stephen moved away with them. How to get out of the theatre without being seen? I dare not wait, in case the door was about to be locked for the night. Praying no one would see me emerge from the dark kitchen, I slipped out and joined the end of the group. To my intense relief there was no sign of either Stephen or Laurence, and after a breathless "Good night" to the others, I hurried through the shadowed alleyway to the car. Perhaps they had reason to be suspicious of Carl. "I know more than you think," he had told me. Presumably the "old dame" referred to Madame Lefevre, but I couldn't begin to imagine how she fitted into the puzzle.

My hands were icy on the steering wheel. If only there was someone I could confide in, someone I could trust completely. I garaged the car and steeled myself for the walk in the darkness round to the front of the house. One of these days I might remember to bring a torch with me. The wind was getting up again, sighing through the branches overhead and sending little eddies of dried leaves swirling round my feet. My footsteps quickened until I was almost running and just as I reached the corner of the west wing someone came quickly round it and cannoned straight into me. I gave a gasp which was more like a strangled scream and struggled furiously to free myself from the grip in which I was held.

102

"Ginnie! Ginnie, is it you? For pity's sake!" The voice penetrated my understanding and in the darkness I could just make out Marcus's face peering down at me.

"Good grief, girl! You told me you were nervous of the dark, but I didn't realize it turned you into a gibbering idiot! Who did you think I was, for Pete's sake? King Kong?"

Shakily I gathered together the shreds of my dignity. "Sorry, Marcus, you startled me, that's all."

"*Startled* you! I shouldn't like to see you really frightened! Come on, I'll walk back to the door with you."

He waited while my rubber fingers struggled to fit the key in the lock. "Any further word from your lord and master?"

"He's coming down for the first night on Thursday. He wants me to go with him."

"You're not going? Good God, Ginnie, you let him walk all over you. Come with me instead, and tell him to go to hell!"

"He says he has some business to discuss. I'd better see him."

"Divorce proceedings?"

My heart lurched. That was one interpretation I had completely overlooked. I said with difficulty, "Perhaps. Thanks for walking back with me, Marcus. Good night." And before he could say anything else, I shut the door. Divorce? A wave of despair welled up and broke over me, buffeting me mercilessly. I had refused all Carl's tentative overtures. Perhaps he was not prepared to try again. And even if he did, how could I go back to that unbalanced life with its continual insecurities and the suspicion which, however hard I combated it, would almost certainly never again leave me in peace while there were women like Leonie Pratt fawning round my husband?

Agonizingly, standing there trembling in the tiny green and white hallway, I resolved to agree to a divorce if that was what Carl wanted. Theatrical marriages were notoriously short-lived. Why should I have imagined my own to be any different?

Chapter 8

SPENT most of the Sunday at the theatre, since I was afraid of alerting Stephen to further suspicion if I suddenly stopped going. "She might have been sent ahead to spy out the land." I wondered if there was some obvious solution to the whole thing that I had unaccountably overlooked, but after a night of restless tossing and turning I was no nearer finding it. The fact that Carl seemed to be involved in some way filled me with dread, since to my illogical way of thinking that effectively cut me off from what I had all along been considering my last emergency line of defence—the police.

That afternoon, in my customary seat with Kitty, I became aware of someone humming softly in the row behind us, and my temples started to pound as I recognized the tune —"Roses of Picardy." It was obviously a test of nerves and I braced myself to withstand it.

Kitty glanced over her shoulder and whispered, "Do shut up, Steve." He leaned forward, his head between ours. " 'I do perceive it hath offended you. Pardon me, sweet one.' "

"Shut up, I'm trying to listen."

He said softly, "Does it offend you too, Ginnie?"

"Not really, though it does make it harder to concentrate on the play. And I won't pander to you with the obvious quotation, either," I added steadily above the clattering of my heart.

He laughed. " 'The food of love'? Well-resisted! You know the tune though, don't you?"

"A bit before my time," I replied, marvelling at my steady voice. " 'Moonlight and Roses,' isn't it?"

"Not quite, try again."

Kitty said in a fierce whisper, "Steve, if you won't be quiet, I shall have to go and sit somewhere else."

"Okay, okay." He sat back and a few minutes later got up and walked down the aisle in time for Sebastian's cue. I drew a long, shuddering breath of relief. Now that Stephen and I had embarked on an almost declared war of nerves it would be safer not to spend so much time at the theatre after all, and I resolved to stay away until the opening on Thursday.

On Monday evening, therefore, I arrived back at the Beeches earlier than I had been doing and Sarah tapped on her window and beckoned me up. The front door was on the latch, presumably ready for Andrew's homecoming, and I went up the stairs to find her waiting at the top.

"I've just put the kettle on. You'll stay for a cup of tea, won't you? I haven't seen you for ages. What have you been doing with yourself?"

I explained about my commitment at the theatre and she was most intrigued. "Andy and I must go along one night. Isn't it shocking, we've lived here for three years and I didn't even know there was a Little Theatre. And you seem to have tracked it down after about three days!"

Less than that, actually, I reflected wryly, taking the cup and saucer she handed me.

"Seen any more of M.M.?" she asked, pushing across the sugar basin.

I smiled. "He frightened the life out of me the other evening, suddenly materializing in the dark."

"Yes, I imagine that could be one of his specialties."

"Oh, come on, Sarah. I told you what he really does for a living."

"All the same—" She looked at me quickly under her lashes. "Am I speaking out of turn?"

"Of course not, why?"

"Well, he did seem to fancy you at the party and you told me about having lunch with him."

"That was quite unpremeditated, I assure you."

"From your point of view, perhaps."

"Sarah, what is this?"

She said slowly, "I rather think he knows a lot more about your movements than you imagine."

"Marcus does?" I stared at her, a creeping coldness spreading up my back.

"Ginnie, it sounds silly but I think he's been following you. I'm almost sure of it. On at least three occasions he came hurrying out of his flat as soon as you'd gone and drove quickly after you. You know he keeps his car at the door except at night. When I noticed it, I started to look out for you coming back—and sure enough he's never far behind you."

I knew for a fact he had followed me to the Picardy that

107

first Sunday. I said jerkily, "Well, I hope he enjoys himself. I don't do anything very exciting."

"I'm sorry if I've alarmed you, but I thought you ought to know."

"Yes. I'm just grateful I have nothing to hide." That was the irony of it, really. They were obviously all suspicious of me—Stephen and Laurence, Rachel, even Carl—and now Marcus. And all for nothing. If I *did* know anything of importance, I couldn't imagine what it was.

Back in my own flat I resolved to test Marcus's interest in my comings and goings. I cooked myself a meal, forced myself to eat it and then, armed at last with a torch, I let myself out of the flat, being careful to let the door close with an audible bang. The light from Marcus's window shone down onto the gravel making a pool of brilliance that I had to cross. As I did so, I was momentarily aware of a shadow other than my own falling across it, and felt a little tingle of excitement. The bait had been taken. Marcus's car was still in the forecourt; perhaps he had been expecting me to go out again.

With the beam of the torch to guide me, I went round to the garages, got the car out and drove slowly onto the road, my mind moving swiftly ahead. I turned left, remembering the flicker of movement I thought I had noticed the other morning, and drove out of the square. Once round the corner, I put my foot down on the accelerator, went quickly down the length of Grove Street and then, coming to the poorly lit turning on the left which I had remembered, turned into it and drove some way along before stopping the car. With my hands tight on the wheel I stared into the driving mirror. I had not long to wait. Two minutes later, Marcus's car passed the end of the road, unmistakable under the light of the street lamp. Sarah had been right. I turned the car and slowly drove home. Once there, I took a pad of writing paper out of the desk and wrote in the middle of the page:

> I shall be going to the office every day this
> week from nine till five. As far as I know, I
> shall not be out in the evening until Thursday.
> I trust this advance notice of my movements
> will save you any unnecessary vigilance.

I dropped it, folded once, through his letter box on my way out the next morning, and that evening he was watching out for me coming home and had reached my front door before I did.

"Ginnie, may I speak to you? I seem to have a bit of explaining to do."

"I'm not interested in your explanations, Marcus," I said coldly. "I strongly resent being followed and if you continue to do so, I shall report you to the police." Brave, and had he but known, empty words.

"Ginnie, please!" He caught hold of the door as I was about to close it, a mixture of embarrassment and quizzical amusement on his face. "All right, I had no right whatsoever to follow you and I apologize, but you are the most intriguing young woman, you know."

"I've no idea what you're talking about."

"In the first place, you weren't who you said you were.

Then there was that curious business about that crummy hotel. You went as white as a sheet when it was mentioned at the Fosses' and as soon as the party was over you shot off there immediately. And there's no doubt you were really frightened when I bumped into you the other evening. Why?" He smiled. "There's nothing like a bit of mystery to make a woman exciting. You really can't blame me that my interest was aroused."

"I'm afraid that you simply have an overactive imagination. Now will you please let go of the door. The flat is getting cold."

"Another brushoff?"

"If you like to call it that."

He sighed and released the door. "All right, have it your own way."

However, the disquiet and indignation I had felt about Marcus following me were swallowed up in the much greater apprehension of my coming meeting with Carl. By Thursday evening I was in quite as bad a state of nerves as any of the cast preparing for the first night. Since presumably he would be coming down by car this time, there was no point in taking my own to the theatre and I phoned for a taxi, sitting swaying on the vast back seat as we drove through the familiar dark streets of the town. It was strange to be an outsider at the theatre, one of the onlookers again. Kitty had done more than her share of serving and two other girls whom I did not know were engaged in pouring the coffee. I moved instead to the queue at the bar. A man called Harry whom I'd seen before was on duty there and passed me my glass of sherry. I took it to a seat that gave a good view of the foyer and prepared to wait for Carl.

The second bell had sounded by the time he arrived. He came bounding up the stairs unwinding his scarf and tossed it and his coat to the girl in the cloakroom before striding into the foyer.

"Sorry I'm late," he said briefly. "We'd better go straight in."

The curtains were just moving as we hurriedly took our seats in the front row.

"If music be the food of love, play on, give me excess of it." Roses of Picardy, I thought numbly. Carl thrust a program into my hand but I had no need of it. Half of my mind repeated the text of the play word for word with the actors, the other half was centred exclusively on Carl; his arm on the rest between us, the familiar tang of his after-shave lotion, his general physical nearness, which was as disturbing to me as it had always been. Attuned to him as I was, I was conscious of his only partial concentration on the play, and wondered what was claiming the other half of his attention. Not myself, that much was obvious. "Strictly business," he had said, and that was the way he was going to play it.

There was no interval at the end of Act 1 and with the beginning of Act 2 I sensed his interest begin to stir. Robert Harling, his official reason for being here, was playing Antonio to Stephen Darby's Sebastian. "Though it was said she much resembled me" . . . She did, too, I thought. Joanna Lacy as Viola, tall and strong-featured with her rich brown hair, was a much more likely sister for Stephen than small dark Rachel. My mind wandered backwards. When had Carl and I last sat side by side in an auditorium?

"Do you want a drink, Ginnie?"

I came back to my present surroundings to find the lights

111

going up at the end of the second act. "Will you mind being stared at by the populace?"

He grimaced. "I can thole it, if you can."

I nodded and he guided me out to the foyer, his hand light under my elbow, but even this casual contact was enough to make me long vehemently for the time for us to be alone together when, surely, we should be able to settle everything. In the meantime I made a determined effort at light conversation. "What do you think of Antonio?"

His eyes went quickly to my face. "Why do you ask?"

"I thought you were considering him for Clarence."

"So you did remember that," he said, an odd note in his voice.

"Isn't that why you came down?"

He handed me my glass. "Yes, yes it is. What do you think of him?"

"Good—I think they're all good."

"Yes, it's a pretty high standard."

"Did you speak to Laurence about releasing Robert?"

"In broad terms, yes. He has no objection."

"Joanna said she wishes you could take them all lock, stock and barrel."

His eyes narrowed. "You seem on remarkably good terms with them all."

"Not all of them, actually."

"Oh?" He waited for an explanation but I sipped my drink without replying.

The play unfolded, its complexities were solved and at last it was over. Carl said, "Where's the best place to eat around here?"

"I don't know, really. The George Hotel is probably as good as anywhere."

Margaret Baillie was at the reception desk as we went into the hall. "Miss Durrell! I was wondering how you were getting on. How nice to see you."

"Hello, Mrs. Baillie. May I introduce you to Carl Clements? Carl, Mrs. Baillie, who was very good to me when I first arrived."

Mrs. Baillie's face had flushed. "Carl Clements? Of course! How exciting! I'm delighted to meet you."

Carl made some smooth, conventional reply and led me away. There was a grillroom downstairs, which I felt would be more conducive to an intimate conversation than the large, impersonal dining room I had used before. We went together down the wide carpeted stairs to be met by a waiter and led to a corner table. Carl ordered the meal, after a minimal consultation with me, and then leaned forward, his hands folded on the table.

"Now, Ginnie, I have to know what your connection is with that theatre. How well do you know those people and how did you come to get mixed up in it? It would be as well if you told me the truth."

"I'm not in the habit of lying to you, Carl," I said stiffly. My brief, rosy hopes of a reconciliation faded and were gone. Business he had said, and business he meant. His tone left no room for doubt.

"Well then?" he prompted impatiently.

"I've been helping out in the kitchen, so of course I know them, some better than others."

"And?"

113

"That's all." I stared at him defiantly, willing the tears not to come.

His gaze was locked onto mine. "I hope to God it is."

"What's that supposed to mean?"

"I wish you'd be frank with me, that's all. Why didn't you admit in the first place that you came here because you knew I'd come soon to see Harling? That was why you made straight for the theatre, wasn't it?"

I glared at him furiously. "Of all the arrogant, conceited—! Let's get one thing quite straight. I most emphatically did *not* know you would come. I'd forgotten all about Robert bloody Harling and I didn't remember until I saw his name on a program. Believe me, my only thought was to get as far away from you as possible. If I could have used the passport I would have done, but in this ghastly, male-oriented world I'm not allowed to!"

"I see. Well, you've made it clear enough now. There's no need for any further histrionics. If that wasn't your reason for coming here, I should be grateful if you'd tell me what it was. I assure you I have a very good reason for wanting to know, quite apart from my responsibility as your husband."

I said shakily, "Isn't it a bit late to start talking about responsibility in that direction?"

His mouth tightened but the arrival of the waiter with the avocado pear prevented an immediate reply. As he moved away, Carl said brusquely, "I wasn't intending to get involved in a personal discussion this evening, but since you've brought it up, who was that fellow at the flat the other night?"

"Just a friend," I answered noncommittally.

"He seemed bloody officious to me."

"If you remember," I said coldly, "you were molesting me at the time."

"Molesting! My God, Ginnie—"

I dug the spoon viciously into the firm, creamy flesh of the avocado. "Anyway, what's the point of this catechism? Why should it matter to you how involved I am with Marcus, the theatre or anything else?"

He said tiredly, "I think you know the answer to that."

"You mean you don't like me straying from the fold? I'm supposed to stay meekly at home knitting and arranging flowers, while you leap in and out of bed with whoever takes your fancy?"

"Ginnie!"

I dropped the spoon with a clatter. I hadn't meant to say any of that but I wasn't thinking very clearly and was only aware of a primitive need to lash out, to hurt him as he'd hurt me. His hand shot out and closed bruisingly round my wrist.

"Now just you listen to me." His voice was low, shaking with the effort to control himself. "I knew something like this would happen if we let personal grievances come out, but what I want to say is simply this. You're to keep away from that theatre, do you hear?"

"Why?" I flung at him.

"I'm getting more and more convinced that there's something shady going on and I won't have you mixed up in it."

"Oh, you won't?" I was struggling to free my hand.

"No, I won't. You little fool, can't you just accept that there are some things you shouldn't meddle in?"

115

"If you'd only stop being so mysterious I might have some idea what you're talking about."

"It's safer for you not to know. You'll just have to take my word for it."

I'll never know what made me say it. Probably just an irresistible desire to shake his superiority, his air of knowing more than I did. For whatever reason, say it I did, and the repercussions were immediate and total. "I suppose you're referring to Madame Lefevre?"

I realized my mistake at once. He withdrew his hand from my wrist as though it had burned him. His face whitened and his eyes were unreadable.

He said incredulously, "You know? You? Ginnie, what is this?" And then, his eyes boring into mine, "You little bitch! God, you bloody little bitch!"

There was no point now in trying to retract, to insist that I didn't understand the relevance of Madame's name nor why it should have such violent reactions whenever I mentioned it. In Carl's eyes I was utterly damned, and nothing else mattered.

The waiter hovered over my barely touched plate. "Perhaps madam would prefer something else? Some soup or prawns?"

I shook my head blindly. Carl, seemingly as incapable of speech as I was, gestured for him to take the plates away. After an aeon of silence he said in a low voice, "He's in it too, isn't he? That was the conclusion we came to."

"Oh yes," I said ringingly, uncaring for Marcus's reputation since my own was gone, "he's in it all right."

I looked up and met his eyes, a bright and bitter blue.

116

"Forgive my curiosity," he said, "but which of them was it you knew beforehand?" I stared at him blankly. "Obviously you must have known at least one of them. Was it from the university?"

I shook my head, unsure what he was referring to.

"Honour among thieves!" he said, and his voice cracked.

It was too much. I said in a rush, "Carl, I don't really—"

"Spare me the excuses. At least you can save me the trouble of seeking them out again. Just tell them, will you, that it won't work. They won't get one penny out of it."

The steak had come, fragrant with garlic butter, garnished with mushrooms and tomatoes. I pushed my chair back. "Don't bother to see me home. I'll get a taxi."

He stood up quickly, fumbled in his pocket and dropped a five-pound note on the table. He caught me up on the staircase and his fingers dug into my arm. "Ginnie, get out of it, for God's sake. Now. I won't tell her you're involved. Go away, anywhere, until it's all blown over. If the police do eventually come in, heaven help you."

"I imagine the adverse publicity wouldn't help your career."

"Do you think I care about that? If I really drove you that far, I deserve all that's coming." He didn't let go of my arm until, shivering uncontrollably, I was in the car. Neither of us spoke again until without any help from me he had driven directly to the Beeches. I pushed open the car door and this time he made no attempt to get out with me.

"You will tell them, won't you, that she's not going to pay? There's no point in carrying on with it any longer." He sat staring up at me. "God, Ginnie, I still can't believe—"

"Good night, Carl."

"Goodbye."

Somehow I was undressed and in my dressing gown. The shaking had lessened a little but not enough to enable me to think clearly. Carl's words were a meaningless jumble in my head. The memory of the expression with which he had looked at me across the table turned every bone in my body to water. What in heaven's name did he think I had done?

Helplessly I walked through the flat from one room to another, picking up books and ornaments and laying them down again. The hands of the clock pointed to twelve—twelve-thirty—one. I was very cold and wrapped my dressing gown more tightly round me. It was October now; perhaps I should think about switching the heating on. I didn't know how to go about it. Carl had always seen to such things. I sank to the floor in the middle of the drawing room, my head in my hands. Sometime during that brief and terrible meal our positions had shifted. After my own half-suspicion of his involvement in the mysterious happenings, he now had no doubt about mine. What had happened to us, that we were apparently able to believe such things about each other? His vehement condemnation echoed in the depths of my being.

Sometime later I rose unsteadily to my feet and went through to the bedroom, switching off the lights. I lay down on top of the bed, pulled the quilt over me and stared up at the ceiling. I don't know how long it was before the turmoil of my thoughts subsided enough to allow me to become aware of the light. My eyes swivelled sharply to the long windows at the end of the room. There was a faint chink where the curtains had not properly come together and it was from this gap that the wavering, uncertain glow poked into the room like a probing finger. Silently I slipped off the bed and padded over to the window.

The room behind me was in darkness and as the light moved away a little, I lifted a corner of the heavy curtain and fearfully peered out. At first I could see nothing, then my eyes made out erratic, spasmodic flashes moving about in the darkness of the park, as though someone were flashing a torch to see his way. But why had its light been playing on the windows of my bedroom?

Suddenly, as I stood watching, a dark figure materialized down to my right and with a little clutch of additional fear I pressed back against the window frame. Someone was coming from the Beeches! Had the light been a signal, an assignation? The dark figure merged into the shadows as it swiftly crossed the road and became lost in the greater blackness that was the park. There were no more flashes of light. Nothing moved again, even I, for five, ten minutes or more. Then at last a shadow detached itself into the figure of a man coming back across the road. And at that exact moment, with the timing of expert stage management, the moon slid without warning from behind the clouds and its light, surer and more revealing than the uncertain beam of the torch that had summoned him, shone full onto his face. It was Marcus Sinclair.

Chapter 9

I REMEMBER very little about that Friday. I went into the office, of course—it was my last day there—and mechanically typed out requests for planning permission and particulars of houses. The world was a hostile place and Rachel's sullen, wary face across the room was a constant reminder of the fact.

"And how did our poor little play appeal to the great one?" she had asked obsequiously when I first arrived.

"He was quite impressed," I replied quietly. We barely spoke again. Despite the faint possibility of meeting Marcus, I went to the usual café for lunch. I was counting on the fact that he was unlikely to come after my tone at our last meeting, nor did he, which was fortunate, because superimposed on all the images of Carl which were branded on my brain that day was one of Marcus in the moonlight. At five o'clock Mr. Holding thanked me warmly for my help during the last three weeks and expressed the hope that he might contact me again during the holiday season next year. But I couldn't begin to contemplate next year.

There was as usual a man on the bench opposite when I reached home just after five-thirty. I felt an urgent need of fresh air myself, and was also curious to know how he would react if I suddenly trespassed into his domain. Accordingly I put the car away and went straight out across the road before I could change my mind. Surprisingly, I had never been in the park before. The untidiness of autumn was strewn over it; drifts of golden brown leaves lay scattered on the grass, splashed with the pink spikes of dahlia petals and the dry, rust-red of dying hydrangeas. Acorns and beechnuts littered the paths and crunched under my footsteps and the scent of bonfire drifted in the air.

Slowly, my hands deep in my coat pockets, I walked round the outer perimeter, studying the houses that faced the park on the other three sides of the square. There was a bowling green with a little wooden hut at the far side from the Beeches and further round a rose garden, now dug neatly over with all the bushes pruned and only the occasional vermilion gash of a late flower against the rich brown soil. A gardener, raking over one of the lawns, paused to nod to me as I passed. Then I had completed the circuit and was back opposite the Beeches. And the man who had been sitting on the bench had gone. A pity. I sat down myself instead and stared over the low railings across the road. From this seat bushes screened the main part of the house, but the east wing was clearly visible. In the upper window I could see Stephanie moving about, probably laying the table for the evening meal. Below, the long Georgian windows of my own flat presented their mirrored glass blandly behind the wrought-iron balconies. The sun, low in the sky behind me, reflected prisms of refracted light in a myriad

121

gems of blue, green, red and gold. Not a good time of the day for spying. It would be better in another half hour, when it would be dark enough for the lights to go on inside but too early to draw the curtains.

After a few minutes I got up and went slowly back across the road. "Tell them she won't pay." So Madame Lefevre had been the recipient of the ransom note—but who was the victim? And whom should I tell? I smiled involuntarily at the thought of Stephen's reaction to such a message. She won't pay. I wondered uneasily how kidnappers would react, faced with this ultimatum. "This has dragged on far too long," Laurence had said. Their nerves were being rubbed raw. How many of them were involved? And what would happen if they suddenly collapsed into panic?

"If I really drove you that far, I deserve all that's coming." Trust Carl, I thought resentfully, slamming the oven door shut, to put everything on a personal basis.

Saturday morning. With what dreary inevitability the weekends came round, waking in me a frenzied desire to fill the limitless hours. And now that my job at Culpepper's had finished, the weekdays would be no better. I should have called at the secretarial bureau before this and found myself somewhere else. At least I shouldn't have to bear Rachel's sullen company any longer.

I embarked on a thorough cleaning of the flat and finished by filling the washing machine with the sheets I had taken off the bed. I set the dial, picked up my basket and shopping list, and was actually pulling the front door to behind me when the telephone called me back.

"Miss Durrell? This is Suzanne Grey."

"Good morning." I waited with a flicker of interest. I had not seen her since her outburst at the end of the last production three weeks ago.

"I wonder if you could meet me for a coffee or something?" Her voice was staccato, vibrant with strain. "There's something I have to ask you."

Another one wanting a part in Carl's new play, I thought resignedly. "I'm just going shopping. How about eleven o'clock at McVities?"

"Fine," she confirmed jerkily. "Thanks." The phone clicked. I dropped it back on its rest and went out.

She was there before me, elegant in grey cashmere with a coral blouse showing at the neck and cuffs. Her lovely eyes were hidden behind a pair of huge round sunglasses. "I've ordered coffee," she said, and, after a pause as I seated myself beside her, "It's good of you to come."

"Not at all." I put the full basket on the floor against the wall. "What can I do for you?" I could see that she was trembling and felt a flicker of alarm. Suppose she had hysterics or something? I should be at least partially responsible for her. Her fingers were pleating and unpleating the paper napkin on the plate in front of her.

"As you probably know, I haven't been at the theatre for a while," she began at last, "so I don't know you as well as the others seem to. I—understand you're married to Carl Clements?"

Here we go! I was determined not to help her. "Yes," I said baldly, and waited.

The coffee came and we were both silent until the waitress had moved away. "Oh, God!" She put her fingers against her

123

shaking lips. "I don't know how to say this."

"You want me to speak to him?" I prompted, relenting at her obvious distress. "I'm afraid I really—"

"What?" Her eyes flew to my face. "You mean you know—?" She drew a long, rasping breath, fighting to control herself. "Sorry, speak to whom?"

I stared at her, nonplussed. "Why, Carl. I thought—"

"Oh, Carl." She relaxed, if it could be called that. "No, no, I was only making conversation. Carl Clements doesn't concern me. At least, not directly."

"Then I really don't see—"

"I went to the show last night," she said rapidly, her fingers compulsively folding the napkin, "and afterwards, backstage, Liz Payne was saying that you—that you mentioned—that you'd said you knew Madame Lefevre."

Quite suddenly the whole episode was fraught with danger. Instinctively my eyes went round the small room preliminary to escape. I had learned the hard way that no good came of the mention of that name. Sensing my withdrawal her fingers, long and tapering but as unyielding as steel, closed on my hand. "Miss Durrell, do you know—" her tongue darted out over her lips. "Did you know Etienne as well?"

"Etienne?"

"Her son, Etienne Lefevre."

"I never met him, no. He was killed in a road accident a few months ago."

She shook her head convulsively. "No, no, he wasn't. He was here in Westhampton only four weeks ago."

I said slowly, "You know, I think we must be speaking of

two different people. Laurence said something about having met her daughter—"

"Laurence did?"

Belatedly I remembered I was speaking to Laurence's wife. I went on hastily, "The Madame Lefevre I know certainly had no daughter and her only son was killed in a car crash in France."

She took a quick sip of coffee. The steam from it misted up her glasses and she took them off, polishing them absent-mindedly. Seeing her face bare, I was appalled at the strain written all over it: the mass of tiny lines at the corner of her eyes, the spasmodic twitching of an eyelid, the skin drawn tightly over high cheekbones.

"That's what she *said,*" she answered jerkily. "I know that's what she told people, but it isn't true."

"Then suppose you tell me the truth," I suggested, hardly daring to hope that at last some of the riddle might be explained.

"Look, perhaps we'd better leave it. If you don't know him you can't really help me after all." To my consternation her eyes brimmed with tears. "It was a forlorn hope, anyway."

"Suzanne, I might be able to help, but I have to know the whole story." I was trying to keep the urgency out of my voice. At last it seemed as though I might learn something which would shed a light on the conundrums which had plagued my weeks in Westhampton. I added cunningly, "And it might help you, too, to talk about it. You look as though you've been bottling things up too long."

"Yes." She let her breath out on a shuddering sigh. "You won't tell Laurence I've spoken to you?"

"No."

She stirred her coffee slowly while I waited in an agony of impatience, terrified she might change her mind after all. At last she began slowly, "It all started in July. We—the company, that is—were over in France to attend the St. Luc Drama Festival." I nodded encouragingly. I remembered hearing Carl speak of it at the time. "While we were there, there was a tremendous hue and cry one night, and we gathered that a man had escaped from the local prison."

She paused, fumbled in her bag and drew out cigarettes. Her fingers were trembling so much I thought she would never manage to light one, but she did. "Well, to cut a long story short, we found him some days later hiding in the basement of the dingy little pension where we were staying." Her eyes, protected once more, flickered at me and away. "You realize, of course, that it was Etienne. We were sorry for him; he was like a hunted animal, dirty and unshaven, and that first night we smuggled some food down to him. He —ate it like a ravening dog, tearing it apart with his hands." She shuddered, drew deeply on her cigarette, and continued more calmly, "Well, I don't suppose you've ever been in a comparable position, but you can take it from me that once you've committed yourself to the extent of feeding a starving man, it's not the easiest thing in the world to turn him over to the authorities. He spoke a little English, said his mother lived in London and if he could only get to her—well, you see the position we were in."

She stubbed out the half-smoked cigarette and lit another. "Almost before we knew it, we found we'd agreed to smuggle him back with us. Of course it was madness, but I think we

126

were all a little mad at the time and he was so charming, so —plausible. He was much the same build as Robert and once they'd let him get cleaned up and into one of Robert's suits, the scruffy fugitive was suddenly a man again, presentable, acceptable, and incidentally very attractive."

Her voice shook. "He made some grand promises of payment once we reached England, and talked rather wildly about how incredibly rich his mother was. I don't think any of us took much notice. Fortunately we were travelling by boat and train, which made things rather easier than all the controls at an airport. I don't know exactly how they managed it, Steve and Laurence and Robert, but they did."

"So, you got him safely to England. Then what?"

"We parted at Folkstone and he caught the London train. We didn't expect to hear from him again, but he came down to Westhampton about two weeks later, bringing a wad of ten-pound notes in an envelope." She gave a choke of laughter. "I don't think many of us had even seen one before. That should have been the end of it, but it turned out to be only the beginning, for me."

I waited, scarcely breathing, and after a minute she went on. "There'd been some sort of spark between us right from the start. It strengthened during the journey home, and when he came to the theatre that night he asked if I could slip away and have a drink with him. After that—well, it became a kind of obsession, for both of us I think. He came down at least once a week and stayed at a rather unpleasant little hotel on the outskirts of the town. Its main advantage was that no one asked questions. I slipped away to meet him whenever I could. It went on all through the summer, up

127

until about a month ago." The shaking had started again and she quickly placed her left hand over her right wrist to steady the cigarette.

"I don't know what happened. That's the god-awful thing. I met him as usual on the Wednesday evening and arranged to go back on the Thursday, but when I got there he'd cleared out—simply vanished. The woman said he'd left that morning, 'with another gentleman.' I just couldn't understand it. He'd never have gone off like that without letting me know, and no other gentleman knew he was even in town."

I said with an effort, "He hadn't said anything the previous day which could have given you a lead?"

"No, nothing."

"No mention of anything at all that was different from usual?"

"No. Oh, he did mention he'd hit another car outside the town, but he hadn't stopped. Obviously he couldn't afford to start exchanging names and addresses, being in the country illegally. But that couldn't have had anything to do with his disappearance, surely?"

I shook my head. There was a kind of numb resignation in my acceptance of this. Obviously my tie-up with the whole thing had been inevitable even before I reached Westhampton. In my mind's eye I saw the Fiat hurtling out of sight and Mrs. Baillie bending anxiously over me. That, had Carl but known it, had been the direct reason for my coming to Westhampton. I moistened my lips.

"And that's all?"

"Almost. I was frantic, of course. When a week had passed

without any word and he didn't return to the hotel, I went to London and called on his mother. I looked up the address in the phone book, but I didn't dare phone, not knowing who might answer."

"What happened?"

"Oh, at first she denied everything, but eventually she asked me in and listened to what I had to say. And finally —Lord, it was unbelievable, Miss Durrell, like a bad movie —she produced a typewritten note demanding money with menaces—isn't that the phrase?"

I said carefully, "You've still no idea where he is?"

"None!" she answered wildly. "He did mention once that he'd run into someone he knew from prison. I imagine they must have taken him, knowing his mother had money. But she was so hard, so unbelievably hard! She was convinced that Etienne himself had a hand in it, to get more money out of her. I tried to convince her he wouldn't have gone without letting me know if he'd had the chance to, but she wouldn't listen. Ranted on about his being a black sheep all his life, in and out of prison and always touching her for money. But if he couldn't go to her, his own mother, who could he turn to? And she said he'd made her life a misery since he came to London, demanding more and more money, and she'd decided it had to end and he wouldn't get any more."

After a long silence, I asked tentatively, "You never mentioned to anyone at the theatre that you were meeting him?"

She threw me a look of contempt. "Do you take me for a fool? Laurence would have killed me, and Steve—"

"Steve?"

She said flatly, "Stephen Darby is always nagging at me

129

to go to bed with him. If he found out someone else had succeeded where he'd failed, I imagine he could be quite nasty about it. But it couldn't be anyone from the theatre who's responsible! Is that what you're thinking? No, you're wrong. It must be one of his French acquaintances. It's just not knowing that's driving me crazy. And then when I heard that you'd mentioned Madame, and also that you were married to Carl Clements and that he'd been down here this week —well, I wondered if she'd contacted him and he had come down to see if he could find out anything. But obviously I jumped to the wrong conclusion. I'm sorry to have burdened you with all this."

"He's in it too, isn't he?" Carl had said, and I'd thought he was referring to Marcus again. Suzanne was probably more right than she knew.

"What had he been in prison for?" I asked, not that it mattered.

"Drug peddling. Not very pleasant, I grant you, but lucrative. That's really all that counts with Etienne. I've no illusions about him. But I still love him, heaven help me. Can you understand that?"

"What are you going to do now?" I asked quietly.

"What can I do? Nothing at all. Go mad, probably." She stood up abruptly, tall and slim in the faultless grey trousers. "Thanks for hearing me out. I'm trusting you to keep it all in confidence."

"I'm sorry not to have been of more help," I replied, but she was already halfway across the room. I hadn't told her of the phone call. It might well have driven her over the edge of hysteria, but obviously either Stephen or Laurence had

130

found out about the affair and, presumably with each other's help, had engineered the whole thing. Rachel had been brought in principally, I imagined, to see to the feeding of the prisoner, though as things turned out Stephen would have had to have taken over while she was incapacitated. It seemed unlikely that anyone else at the theatre was in on the secret. They had all reacted to the name of Lefevre because they had all been involved in bringing him into the country, but only Stephen, Laurence and Rachel had extra reason to be wary of me.

I signalled to the waitress for another cup of coffee. At least I now knew the identity of the man from Room 127. I knew, even if I could not prove, who had typed the ransom note and who had received it. I also understood why Carl had questioned me so closely about my coming to West-hampton and my connection with the theatre. Obviously, as Suzanne had guessed, Madame had consulted Carl after her visit. It may have been because of his connection with the theatre—and although she couldn't have known it, his exist-ing interest in Robert Harling had provided the perfect cover for his coming; or it may have been that Carl had over the years been more like a son to her than her own. She obviously idolized him, and for our part we had both been very fond of the old lady. Carl had good cause to be grateful to her for her backing of productions for him before he became so well-known.

I wondered again whether I now had sufficient informa-tion to go to the police. At least I knew Carl wasn't crimi-nally involved, but the implications of the whole affair had escalated alarmingly. If I did report it, Etienne would be sent straight back to France, merely exchanging one prison for another, but Laurence and Stephen would face heavy sentences themselves and the whole group be severely penalized for smuggling Etienne into the country. There would be unpleasant publicity all round, for the theatre, which obviously would have to close, for Madame Lefevre, and probably also for Carl. And the ironic thing was that Madame did not want her son back anyway. I knew she would never have gone so far as to turn him over to the police, but she was nonetheless glad to be relieved of the embarrassment of his presence. It began to look as though going to the police would help nobody and there was always the possibility that in the ensuing panic Etienne might come to real physical harm. All in all, by far the most satisfactory solution seemed to be to find out exactly where he was and set him free myself. The incredible simplicity of it stunned me. Laurence and Stephen, who seemed badly frightened by the misfiring of their plan, would feel only relief, knowing Etienne was in no position to report them; the theatre crowd would come to no harm at least as a direct result of any action of mine, and as far as I was concerned, Etienne and Suzanne could do whatever they liked.

I became aware that all round me people were now eating lunch, and that the waitress, judging by her expression, did not approve of my long-drawn-out cups of coffee. To pacify her, and avoid having to disrupt my thoughts at that juncture, I ordered an omelette and more coffee.

The obvious place for them to be holding him was the theatre. In all probability, Stephen and Rachel had come straight from him that afternoon when I hid on the staircase.

Excitement began to move in me. All that remained was to discover which of those rooms farther along the passage or under the stage was the one that concealed him, how many keys were in existence and who had charge of them, and the best way, once these obstacles had been overcome, to remove Etienne from the theatre without being seen. As a first step, I would go along to the theatre that afternoon. The more frequently I dropped in, the less notice anyone would take of my presence, and I could begin to inch my way towards the hidden regions at the back of the building.

At last, and to the waitress's obvious if unspoken relief, I left the café. The afternoon had turned cool and windy. I put the full shopping basket on the back seat of the car and drove quickly to my usual parking place. It was not until I actually reached the theatre that I realized a performance was in progress. The Saturday matinee; I'd forgotten all about it. Not that it mattered. All I had to do today was to re-establish my presence there.

I looked into the kitchenette, but tea was well under way for the approaching interval. That seat across the foyer was where I had sat to wait for Carl. For a moment I was tormented by a wave of longing to run to the nearest phone box and call him, explain my innocence in the whole affair and stop him thinking such unspeakable things about me. I fought it down. Soon, when I had found out all I had to know, I would be able to go to him and present him with the complete picture. After that—but I couldn't think beyond that.

A hum from the auditorium indicated that the curtain had fallen at the end of Act 2 and the audience began to spill out

133

into the foyer. It contained a large proportion of schoolchildren; perhaps *Twelfth Night* was on the local schools' syllabus this year. Glasses of fruit squash were lined up on the counter as an alternative to tea.

"Hello, Ginnie. Can't you keep away?" Liz Payne had appeared smilingly at my side.

"Of course not. Anything I can do?"

"I don't think so. I just came in to hear the general comments. Did it go all right the other night? There was quite a good write-up in the local paper."

"I thought it was very good, yes."

She glanced sideways at me. "I hear Mr. Clements has invited Robert to appear in *Richard the Third* with him. Everyone's green with envy!"

"Yes, he's had him in mind for some time."

"I was glad to see you together on Thursday—" Her voice trailed off uncertainly.

"Our togetherness," I said crisply, "was purely academic."

"Oh. I'm sorry."

"Cup of tea?" I thrust one into her hand. "How are things backstage?"

"Much as usual. Unfortunately Suzanne's back in evidence and she's such a bag of nerves, even though she's not in the play, that she infects everyone else."

A bell sounded and people began to push past us to replace their cups and glasses on the counter.

"I'd better go and hook Joanna into her costume. Are you staying for the next act?"

"I'll probably watch it for a while."

134

I had thought there might be a chance of finding my way behind the scenes while Laurence and Stephen were occupied onstage, but it immediately became evident that the girl on duty in the cloakroom had the bend in the passage clearly in view, and might well wonder what I was up to if I disappeared along it, especially since she didn't know me. There was nothing more I could do today, and after watching the play for some time from just inside the auditorium, I slipped out quietly and drove back home. At least between them Suzanne and the theatre had passed a sizable portion of the day for me.

Chapter 10

MY thoughts were still revolving round all the new facts I had learned from Suzanne, and when I pushed open the front door of the flat, it was a moment before I fully registered the impact of what met my eyes. Water was lying at least two inches deep all over the hall carpet and from the kitchen a strange, rhythmic grating reached me which, panic-stricken, I immediately associated with the washing machine I had switched on before going out that morning.

Frantically I waded through to survey the chaos in the kitchen. Water was still gushing from the pipe connecting the machine to the wall, while the machine itself jerked and vibrated alarmingly. Closing my mind to the probable condition of the sheets inside it, I splashed across and switched it off. The next priority was obviously the mains water tap, but here my desperate attempts proved useless. It was jammed solid and none of my frantic wrenches moved it one iota. I tore open one drawer after another, searching for a spanner, pliers, any of those mysterious implements with which Carl seemed able to ward off any emergency. There was nothing. I turned flounderingly, the water swirling round my legs, and waded out of the kitchen. The water was seeping out of the open front door onto the gravel, and in that moment Marcus came quickly into view. I had never been more glad to see him.

"Ginnie, what in the name of heaven—?"

"It's the washing machine. The mains tap is jammed and although the machine's turned off now, the water still keeps coming."

As I spoke, he was swiftly removing shoes and socks and rolling up his trouser legs. Within seconds he had reached the stubborn tap, wrestled with it, and won. The water stopped with a last mournful drip and we turned together to assess the extent of the damage. I said tremulously, "I don't know where to start!"

"Buckets," he said crisply, "buckets, mops, and all the cloths you can lay your hands on. Have you a broom? You start to sweep the water out of the front door while I tackle this room. Will it have got in anywhere else, do you think?"

"There's a raised threshold outside the bedroom and drawing room doors. I don't think it's reached that high."

"Well, don't open the doors, for Pete's sake, till we've got the level down a bit."

A quick search revealed only one bucket and the washing-up bowl. Marcus handed one to me and the great clear-up got under way. My main concern was the state of the emerald carpet in the hall. It made a sickening, squelshing sound as I walked over it mopping and squeezing, mopping and

137

squeezing. At the end of an hour Marcus had restored the kitchen and bathroom more or less to normal and came to see how I was progressing.

"I think we ought to have that done professionally," he commented. He glanced at his watch. "It's five o'clock now. No one would come and collect it at this time on a Saturday, but if we roll it up in towels and take it along, they'll do something, surely. Have you any old towels?" I shook my head. "Then get plain white ones. If the dye comes off on them, at least they're easier to replace than the carpet." He knelt down and felt round the edges just inside the door. "Thank heaven it's such a small hall. You kneel the other side and we'll roll it up very slowly, keeping level. Move the telephone table, will you?"

Ten minutes later the sodden carpet, protected by towels, was in the boot of his car. Wearily I watched him drive away and turned disconsolately to survey the bare boards of the hall. Only then, with fingers crossed, did I dare to open the doors to the other rooms. To my overwhelming relief, all was well. Except for a damp patch just inside, the carpets in the bedroom and drawing room were dry. I went back into the damp kitchen and automatically started to unpack the basket of groceries I'd dropped on the table when I first came in. Then I stuffed newspaper inside my wringing shoes, vainly hoping they weren't ruined beyond repair, and changed out of my soaked skirt. I had just hung it in the airing cupboard when Marcus came back.

"All right, they'll do it. They seem reasonably optimistic about the result. It may be pricey, but worth it, I imagine. How are the other rooms?"

"All right, thank goodness. Marcus, I can't begin to thank you for all your help." Especially after my attitude last time we met, I thought with embarrassment.

"Don't mention it. One thing you can do, though. Come up and have dinner with me. You don't want to crash up and down the bare boards here all evening and you look as though you could do with relaxing while someone else does the work."

In the circumstances I could hardly refuse. He lit the central heating boiler for me to help dry out the damp floor boards and add a little comfort and then I went with him up the stairs to his own flat. Being in the main building, it was a different layout from mine. A small kitchenette was separated from the main sitting room by a breakfast bar and the bedroom and bathroom were at the back. "It suits me admirably," he remarked, handing me a drink. "I can still watch the telly while I prepare a meal!"

The sitting room was obviously male-orientated. A deep leather sofa stood comfortably on one side of the fireplace, there were dark red easy chairs, an open desk littered with papers and, to one side of the window, a drawing board with plans pinned on it. In the fireplace an electric fire with mock logs flickered cosily, its red shadows reflected on the ceiling.

"Now, the menu tonight is either goulash or coq au vin!"

I turned in astonishment. "Good heavens, don't tell me you're a cordon bleu cook!"

He smiled. "People, especially women, seem to imagine that left to themselves men will exist on tinned steak and baked beans. Quite wrong, you know. We usually have one *pièce de résistance* that we bring out for company and for the rest, well, it's simpler to make a big casserole of some sort that will last for most of the week. That's the way I work it, anyhow. There's some of Wednesday's goulash left and I bought a frozen chicken this morning, hence the alternative."

"The goulash sounds wonderful. I'm most impressed."

"I once became involved in a culinary discussion with our two artistic friends in Flat Four—it was quite illuminating. They even go so far as a lace tablecloth and candlesticks!"

"That I can believe," I said drily.

"I have to confess that cork mats and a bottle of plonk are more my style, but they're nice mats, views of old London. Anyway, presumably you're not ready to eat yet; it's only just after six. Finish your drink and I'll pour you another."

He switched on a lamp beside the fireplace and its soft glow lit the surrounding area, leaving the rest of the room in shadow. "Excuse me a moment while I go and change. These clothes are more than a little damp. There are magazines under the coffee table."

I bent forward to retrieve a couple, that week's *Punch* and a current edition of *Autocar,* but I didn't open either. I was very tired, mentally and physically, and it was pleasant to lie back in the luxurious depths of the sofa and let my eyes move lazily over the comfortable outlines of the room. If only Marcus had not followed me, had not made that moonlit excursion to the park, I could have relaxed still more.

"A penny for them!" I hadn't noticed his return and his voice made me jump. He had changed into a light-coloured polo neck shirt and slacks and the immediate effect was to make him look younger. I had never seen him in casual clothes before.

140

"Well? What were you thinking about?"

"Nothing in particular," I hedged.

"In other words, mind my own business!" He sat down opposite me, settling back in the folds of the chair so that his face was in shadow. "That was the answer I expected, of course, though I haven't given up hope that one day you'll tell me exactly what's going on. Personally I can't decide whether it's diamond smuggling or espionage!"

I said with an effort, "Don't be silly, Marcus."

"Then at least tell me why you're under constant surveillance from that seat in the park."

My hands tightened convulsively round the cold glass. "I was hoping," I said carefully, "that you could tell me."

"And what is that supposed to mean?"

"Only that if you're in the park at dead of night yourself, you should presumably know what other people are doing there."

There was a silence, punctuated by the steadily ticking grandfather clock in the shadows and a faint hissing from the fire. He said quietly, "You don't miss much, do you?"

"I can't afford to."

"Then I'll tell you. I went over there to find out what the hell was going on. A torch beam had been moving over the window and I decided the time had come to get to the bottom of it all."

"And did you?"

"No. Whoever it was vanished into thin air." There was another long silence before he added, "Do you believe me?"

"I'm not sure."

He moved impatiently. "I suppose that stupid Foss woman has been filling your head with more nonsense. I have to admit with all due respect that she irritates me profoundly. I don't doubt it was she who told you I was following you?"

I didn't reply but he went on, "Well, I explained about that. Hell, Ginnie, I lead a dull, rather lonely life, and when someone like you appears close at hand, and wrapped in mystery to boot, of course I'm interested, and not a little concerned for your welfare." He stood up abruptly and poured himself another drink. "So you see," he went on brittly, "there's no mystery as far as I'm concerned. I just happen to fancy you more than somewhat, and from my angle it's one hell of a drag that you're still so hung-up on that husband of yours. And if that's any of Sarah Foss's damn business, you have my permission to tell her." He drained his glass and added more calmly, "Sorry, I didn't mean to say that."

I had no choice but to believe him. After all, I'd never been able to see how he fitted in with the kidnapping, and his reasons for such intervention as he had made were plausible enough; all of which, while it settled my mind in one direction, gave rise to an entirely new problem of a more personal nature. This quiet, softly lit room, allied with my own extreme lassitude, was not the ideal setting in which to resolve it.

The silence lengthened between us and I steeled myself to break it. "Please don't ask me any more, Marcus. There is something, of course, it's pointless to deny it, but it's not my secret and I can't tell you. Actually, I rather wish I could."

He was standing looking down at me during this stiff little speech, but again, since he was above the lamplight, I couldn't see the expression on his face.

142

"One last question, then. Does your husband fit into it at all?"

"Vaguely."

"So the business he wanted to discuss with you wasn't divorce?"

"No."

He seemed about to say something else, then changed his mind. "How was the play?"

"It went off very well."

"And the Master was impressed?" He didn't seem able to keep the sarcasm out of his voice when he referred to Carl. I remembered Carl's opinion of him—"bloody officious."

"He was, yes," I replied steadily.

"I'm surprised you didn't go back with him. Or is he leaving you here to do the dirty work for him?"

"Marcus—"

"Sorry, I've exceeded my quota of questions, haven't I? I'll shut up and put a record on instead." He walked quickly over to the stereo set and a moment later the quiet room had settled back into a listening silence as music throbbed from the dark corners. We sat in almost complete silence for the next twenty minutes or so, our thoughts swirling and dipping aimlessly against the background of the music. When the record at last ended, I turned my head to find Marcus watching me. "You know," he said softly, "there's a restful quality about you, with that wide brow and smooth hair. You've been on edge ever since I met you, but it still shines through. I can quite see the attraction you must have for Clements, surrounded as he is by all that synthetic glamour. You remind me of the old song, 'You'd be so nice to come home

143

to.' " He gave a short laugh. "And that, lady, is dangerous thinking, believe me! I'd better go and see to the meal."

"Can I help?" I asked a little awkwardly.

"Certainly not. This is your evening off. You might turn the record over, though."

I did so, then wandered over to the window. It was strange to look out on a different view of the park and from a greater height. Lights showed in the windows of the houses at the far side. I wondered with a tremor of apprehension whether a vigilant figure was still concealed in the shadows. It was oddly comforting to know that Marcus was after all concerned for my safety. I looked across at him as he moved about the kitchen, aware of a faint regret. He had been astute in deploring my continuing fixation about Carl. Without that safeguard I knew I would have been attracted to him.

"Why did your wife divorce you?" I asked suddenly, without stopping to think. His hand paused fractionally over the rice pan and I said quickly, "I'm sorry, Marcus, I've no right whatever—"

"It's all right." He carried the pan to the sink and poured the contents into a colander. The kitchen was as tidy and spotless as a ship's galley, despite the dinner preparations in progress. I wondered for a moment whether he had taken my apology as a negation of the question, but he went on, "Incompatibility, really. Not that it's called that over here. I think the term is 'irretrievable breakdown' of the marriage. Same thing, at least in our case."

"Does it upset you to talk about her?"

"Not in the slightest. We married very young and for all the wrong reasons. She was pretty, gay, sociable; I was stu-

144

dious, quiet and home-loving. Hopeless."

He brought the dishes round the end of the counter and laid them on mats on the mahogany table. "And added to all that, I was studying for exams and she just couldn't understand that we couldn't go dancing every night. Oh, it was largely my fault, I suppose. I wasn't prepared to make allowances when she behaved like a spoiled child. It got to the stage when I dreaded going home at night."

"I'm sorry," I said quietly.

"I suppose it's because of Angela that I don't care for Mrs. Foss. She's much the same type, chattering endlessly, irresponsible, the eternal little girl. It leaves me cold."

"I think you're being rather unfair to Sarah."

"No doubt, but I can't see it worrying her. She's probably convinced that I murdered my wife, anyway." He passed me a plate of steaming goulash. "The fact of the matter is that I'm a thoroughly unsociable devil and never at my best with women anyway. I just can't seem to relax with them, somehow."

"You seem pretty relaxed now."

"Yes," he said briefly, "that was the point I made earlier. Would you like to help yourself to rice?"

We ate in silence for a while and then, apropos the goulash, started talking about Europe and the places we had visited. It seemed the safest topic we had found yet and I prolonged it as much as possible. We had fruit and cheese and Marcus made an enormous jug of coffee which we carried back to the fire. The music still played sensuously in the background and I knew it would not be wise to stay much longer. There were lengthening gaps now in the conversation

145

and the warmth and food had made me sleepy. At last, reluctantly, I stood up. Across the hearth Marcus also rose to his feet. I said, "Marcus, it's been lovely, but—"

He took two steps towards me and without conscious thought I was in his arms, my treacherous body instantly responsive after its long abstinence from Carl. At some level of consciousness I was ashamed of the pleasure Marcus's kisses were giving me, at another more basic level I wanted them never to stop. Without warning, reason suddenly asserted itself and I wrenched my mouth free of his. "Marcus, I must go—I have to—" His hands dropped away. His breathing was ragged and uneven. After a moment he said flatly, "If you must, you must."

"I'm sorry," I whispered.

"Well, don't cry!" he said harshly. "All I ask is, don't cry."

He moved quickly away and stood staring out of the window with his hands driven deep down into his pockets while I tried weakly to marshal what resources I had to enable myself to regain the lonely safety of my own flat. God help me, I wanted to stay.

Over by the window Marcus made a sudden startled movement. "Ginnie, come here." I hurried across and he put a hand on my shoulder. "Look, down to the left." His voice was taut with excitement. "Do you see? There's someone on your balcony!"

I stiffened under his hand. "Oh no!" But I too could see the flutter of movement against the white painted scrollwork. From this angle only the near corner of the drawing-room balcony was visible. Marcus turned suddenly.

"I'm going down. You stay here."

146

"No, Marcus, you mustn't! Wait till he's gone, please!"

"Nonsense. You're not to move, do you hear?" And the next moment he had disappeared, leaving me trembling at the window with the feel of his kisses still on my mouth.

With held breath I waited long minutes until, down to my left, I saw him emerge and make his way in the shadows of the building round the corner of the wing. After that everything happened at once. There was a scuffle, a muffled shout and then a dark figure vaulted lightly over the balustrade and disappeared into the darkness. Frozen with fear, I waited to see what had become of Marcus. It was endless minutes later that I saw him appear, and gave a little sob of relief. He came back slowly and I saw that he was limping. I turned and sped down the stairs, meeting him at the bottom.

"Marcus, are you all right? What happened?"

"He got away, blast him."

"Are you hurt?"

"Not much." He put a hand up to the corner of his mouth and it came away dark with blood.

"Let me bathe it for you."

"No need; I can manage. Have you got your bag and things?"

"No, I just ran down—"

"Get them, will you?" He leaned against the newel post breathing deeply while I hurried back up the stairs. The music was still playing and the cigarette he'd dropped in the ashtray when I had said I must go home still smouldered there. I grabbed my bag and fled from the room before its tentacles could reach out for me again.

As I rejoined him he silently held out his hand for my key

147

and went ahead of me into the flat. The bare boards in the hall were bleak and unwelcoming, but they were almost dry and the dusty smell of long unused heating met our nostrils. At least the atmosphere was warm. Swiftly Marcus went through every room, opening cupboard doors, bending to look under the bed. He tested the catches on all the windows and checked that the lock on the back door had not been tampered with. When at last he was satisfied, he turned towards me, but he was still not quite meeting my eyes. "Will you be all right here alone?"

"Yes, quite, thank you."

"You wouldn't rather I stayed? In the drawing room, naturally."

"I'll be all right," I repeated tremulously, "but can't I at least bathe that cut for you?"

"It's nothing, I tell you. As long as you're sure, then, I'll go, but if you hear anything, anything at all, ring me and I'll be here inside two minutes. The number's 821—got it?"

"821," I repeated mechanically. "Marcus, thank you so much for—"

"Good night, Ginnie." The door closed behind him on a final little click. I stood in the hall staring at it while the tears rained silently down my face. Then, wearily, I slid the bolt into position.

Suppose, I thought suddenly, going into the bedroom, that I hadn't been with Marcus but in my own flat when the intruder arrived? What would have happened then? The unaccustomed warmth from the radiator was soothing, but it didn't prevent the shivering which had taken hold of me, rattling my teeth with a ferocity that was almost pain. Reac-

148

tion, I told myself judderingly, from all the strains and stresses of the last week, and the emotional maelstrom with Marcus; but I couldn't trust myself to think about Marcus yet; not about Marcus, nor Carl, and certainly not about the unwelcome visitor on the balcony. Zombie-like I moved through the routine of washing and undressing and, with the last ounce of my strength, slid thankfully into bed. I only just managed to reach out a grouping hand to switch off the lamp before sleep, swift, total and overwhelming, claimed me utterly.

Chapter 11

MARCUS phoned soon after ten the next morning. His voice was clipped and businesslike. "Everything all right? No further disturbances?"

"Not a thing, but I slept so heavily it would have taken a lot to wake me."

"You're lucky," he said shortly. "Ginnie, about last night. I'm sorry if I embarrassed you; it won't happen again." He gave a brief laugh. "I imagine you'll be careful in future not to leave your washing machine on. It can land you in deeper water than you realize!"

I started to speak but his voice overrode mine. "The real reason I'm phoning is to let you know I'm going to report the incident to the police. I'm not prepared to accept the responsibility of it."

I said quickly, "Oh, Marcus, please don't! Really, I'm sure it wasn't as serious as you thought."

"It was enough to leave me with a stiff jaw and a wrenched ankle," he said tightly, "which seems to me to go beyond the definition of playing games."

150

"I'm not trying to belittle what you did, I'm very grateful, but I honestly don't think he would actually have hurt me. It's a war of nerves, intimidation." I hesitated. "Did you— were you able to get a glimpse of him?"

"Not so much a glimpse as an impression. It certainly wasn't one of the old fuddy-duddies from the park, I assure you. I wouldn't have had any difficulty catching up with them. This was a young man, tall and strong and for some reason exceptionally anxious that I shouldn't see his face— almost as though he thought he might be recognized."

Stephen, as I'd thought. The men in the park were probably just paid to sit there, without being told why. The more dubious occurrences, the doorbells and torch beams in the night, would have to be Stephen's own responsibility. I couldn't imagine what he hoped to gain by climbing on my balcony, unless it was merely stepping up the terror campaign. I was obviously proving harder to shake off than he'd hoped.

Marcus's voice broke in on my musings. "Ginnie, what the hell am I going to do with you? You won't tell me what this is all about, you won't let me go to the police. Suppose something does happen to you, that you've been under-estimating them, whoever they are. How do you think I'd feel then?"

"I'm hoping that it won't go on much longer now, but there's nothing the police could do except keep an eye on the place."

"At the moment I'd even settle for that. You're not in trouble with them yourself, are you?" His voice had sharpened as the idea suddenly struck him.

"No, of course not."

"Then I can't see why you won't let me contact them. Has anything like this ever happened before?"

"Not exactly like this."

"What was it?"

"My doorbell did ring once, in the middle of the night."

He swore under his breath. "And Carl knows you're mixed up in all this?"

"He knows," I said bleakly and a little unfairly.

"Well, I sure as hell wouldn't allow you to be, in his place, but that's neither here nor there. You do promise to contact me if you're at all worried? You won't let that episode last night stand in the way?"

"I'll contact you."

I went through to the drawing room with a cup of coffee and sat staring disconsolately out of the window. There was no man on the seat this morning. Perhaps, I thought fatuously, they don't work on Sundays. I had a bizarre mental picture of an Intimidators' Association complete with rules and union cards. Moira Francis's two boys were kicking a ball about on the grass and there was a steady downward drift of yellow-brown leaves. In the flat above the whir of a vacuum cleaner rose and fell, creaking its way across my ceiling. It was Sunday morning. Everyone—almost everyone —was relaxing, or catching up with the housework or cooking the roast or going to church. But here and there dotted round the district were those for whom Sundays were no different from other days and offered no letup of tension— Etienne Lefevre, his kidnappers, myself.

"Tell them she won't pay," Carl had instructed, but how could I? If I contacted them, even by the ignoble means of an anonymous telephone call, how would they react? They couldn't know I had decided to do nothing, to let events take their course. They would probably imagine flocks of sirening police cars closing in, and they might be desperate enough to try to silence me more permanently. Perhaps after all I was playing a more dangerous game than I realized. And yet I still balked from believing people I knew socially were capable of murder. Stephen was hard, devious, possibly even vicious, but surely no more, and Laurence, already riddled with doubts, was surely incapable of violence. But a frightened man could sometimes be more dangerous than a cool one, panic reactions couldn't be gauged in advance. It was a temptation to let familiarity breed contempt, to go to Laurence and say, "Look, I know all about it but his mother's not going to pay, so you might as well let him go." Once again the stumbling block was having to convince them that proceedings would not be taken as soon as Etienne was free.

Slowly the hours crawled by. The Francis boys went in for their lunch and later a young couple pushed a pram round the park. The Sunday afternoon film, muted from the set upstairs, provided a background hum to my perusal of the papers. Miserably I found myself wondering with which of our friends Carl would be spending the day. There would be no shortage of invitations. The usual shaft of pain twisted inside me. I was glad when at long last the time came for me to go to bed.

The clarion of the telephone must have been going on for a long time. I lay listening to it as it wove itself neatly into my dreams, but at last its insistence forced me awake and I raced through to the hall and caught it up. "Hello? Yes?"

153

I was met with silence: not the silence of a dead phone, nor of a holding line. Although I could not hear breathing, I was acutely, nerve-tinglingly aware that someone, somewhere, was at the other end of the line, waiting, listening. I dropped it back with a clatter and stood staring down at it, willing it not to ring again. Outside the wind lashed the branches and closer at hand the click of the cooling hall radiator brought my heart to my mouth. The seconds stretched into minutes. The smug black muzzle remained obstinately silent. Teeth chattering, I crept back to bed.

Monday morning, and no job to go to. I almost wished I could go along to Culpepper's as usual, even if it meant bearing with Rachel's moods.

After I had tidied the flat I drove into town and called at the secretarial bureau. "Oh yes, Miss Durrell, your three weeks with Culpepper's are up, aren't they? Now let's see what we have that might interest you. You prefer to work for estate agents, don't you?"

"Not really," I said carefully, and as she looked up, surprised, I added quickly, "If there's nothing in that line, I'm quite happy to try something else."

Her long fingers continued expertly riffling through the card index. "I have a couple here that might appeal. There's a vacancy for a receptionist-cum-secretary at the George Hotel, which could be quite interesting, or—"

"I'll try the George," I said at once. It had been my first home in Westhampton and at least I knew Mrs. Baillie. I felt in need of familiar faces and surroundings at the moment.

A few hours later I was installed behind the desk in the hall. My switch of employment had been accomplished

154

swiftly and painlessly; I was duly grateful. Mrs. Baillie seemed pleased to see me and came over to welcome me to the staff. "By the way," she continued a little awkwardly, "that was *the* Carl Clements, the actor, you were with the other evening, wasn't it? I was almost sure, but it was such a surprise—"

"Yes, it was," I answered briefly.

"How very exciting! I wonder—I don't want to make a nuisance of myself, of course, but I'm on the committee of the Townswomen's Guild this year. Would it—is there the remotest chance that he might agree to come and speak to us?"

"I don't know." I was aware of sounding ungracious and added perfunctorily, "I could ask him if you like." Obviously Mrs. Baillie had not witnessed my precipitate and dinnerless departure from the hotel on Thursday night.

"Would you? I'd be so grateful. It would be wonderful to have a real celebrity like that!" My lack of response finally began to reach her and I could sense her disappointment in holding back all the questions she was longing to ask me. With a little murmur of thanks for my grudging offer, she reluctantly moved away.

The morning passed in a whirl of phone calls, reservations and bookings. It was interesting to see all the different people who came through the swing doors, to note the varying places of residence they wrote in the visitors' book. By lunchtime I was feeling perfectly at home and congratulating myself on my luck in finding the job. And then Marcus came pushing through the swing doors with the strange, shabby little man I had first seen him with. He saw me at once and hesitated, but I was dealing with a queue of people at the desk and he merely nodded and went through to the bar. Soon after that it was time for my lunch and I handed over to Jane, the girl I remembered from my brief stay at the hotel, and made my way downstairs to the staff dining room.

It was as I came back up the stairs that I heard my name called and Marcus, alone now, came out of the grillroom where Carl and I had had our disastrous confrontation. "You do turn up in the most unexpected places!" he remarked with a smile.

"So do you, and with the most unexpected people!"

"Joe? He's the foreman of one of the building firms I work with. If he can't contact me at home, he tries here, knowing I usually drop in for a pre-lunch drink. I supervise the work on behalf of my clients and occasionally queries arise." Wryly I remembered my dark suspicions about the unlikely alliance.

"Are you all right, Ginnie? You look rather drawn."

"I had a disturbed night," I said shortly.

His hand gripped my arm. "Not our friend on the balcony again?"

"No, a phone call. At two A.M."

He made an exclamation under his breath. "What happened?"

"Nothing. No one spoke. How's your ankle, by the way?"

"All right if I don't put too much weight on it. Ginnie, I don't like this at all."

We had reached the hall. "I must go; I'm due back on duty."

"What time will you be home?"

156

"About five-thirty, I should think."

"Right, I'll call round for a few minutes then, if I may. I've just had an idea which might be worth considering."

I nodded and went back to the desk. Phone calls in the dark hours or not, I was determined to go to the theatre that evening and make a positive attempt to locate Etienne Lefevre.

I was in the middle of preparing my evening meal when Marcus called and he followed me into the kitchen and sat down at the table, accepting the glass of sherry I had poured ready for him.

"What's this idea you mentioned?" I asked, turning down the light under the vegetable pan.

"Simply this. You sleep in my flat and I'll sleep here."

I turned sharply and stared at him.

"Look, honey, whatever you might say, I think you're in danger. I still feel I ought to get in touch with the police, but you're so set against it, so this seems a good way round it. No one will know about the arrangement, of course. We make the switch after dark and again early in the morning, before anyone's around, so we're back in our own flats for breakfast. You'll be quite safe up there and I'll be on hand to deal with any funny little games they might try."

I said awkwardly, "Marcus, I can't let you do all this for me. You've already had your face bruised and twisted your ankle. Suppose you get really hurt next time?"

"I thought you insisted there was no real danger?"

"I don't really think there is, but I suppose there's always the possibility."

"Exactly," he replied grimly, "and rather me than you.

Don't worry, I can take care of myself now that I have their measure. What do you say, shall we try it?"

The thought of Marcus's flat, safely away from creeping footsteps and balconied windows, was irresistible. "If you're sure you don't mind."

"That's fine, we can put it into effect straightaway. I'll go back and change the sheets and things. You stay here till I come and I'll see you safely up to my flat. What time would suit you?"

"Well, I have to go to the theatre tonight, so—"

He frowned. "Again?"

"I'm afraid so."

"What time will you get back?"

"It shouldn't be long after ten." Provided no one finds me prowling in the passages. I gave an involuntary little shudder and his eyes narrowed.

"Ginnie, is it something to do with the theatre, all this business?"

I didn't reply and he went on softly, "Of course! I should have guessed before. You've been spending nearly all your time there." He sipped his drink, his eyes still intent on my face. "Then I'd better come with you. It's certainly not safe for you to go alone."

"Marcus, it's sweet of you, but no. I must go by myself. There's something I have to find out."

"Can't I help you?"

"Not really, no."

"I wish I could get my hands on that husband of yours!" he said with sudden violence. "When I think of the calm way he sits back and lets you take all these risks—"

158

"No," I said again, and my voice wasn't steady. "He's no idea that I might be in danger. You have to believe that."

"How can I believe it? He knows you're here, that—"

"He thinks," I said clearly, "that I'm one of them."

Marcus looked at me blankly. "One of who? The crowd who is trying to scare you?"

"Yes. It's too long a story to go into now, but I couldn't let you go on thinking that about Carl."

"Damn Carl!" he said in a low voice. "Whatever he knows or doesn't know, damn him just the same!"

I smiled crookedly. "Yes. Well, anyway—"

"All right, so I'm not even to be allowed to go to the theatre with you. One thing I will insist on, though. You're not to take your car round to the garage when you get back. Leave it at the door and when I've seen you into my flat I'll go and put it away."

"Thank you," I said meekly.

He looked at me for a moment, then pushed his chair back and stood up. "Thanks for the drink and for God's sake take care of yourself. I'll be watching out for you and I'll come down as soon as I hear the car. You'll have to pop in here anyway for your night things." I went with him to the door, feeling the tension in him; I was trembling myself as I went back to the kitchen to drain the vegetables.

The wind had risen again by the time I drove to the theatre, hurling leaves down from the trees and rushing them in eddies and swirls along the gutters. I had timed my arrival for just after the curtain had gone up. The foyer was deserted, but Harry was still behind the bar at the far end, washing glasses and wiping down the counter. He waved to me and

159

I waved back and moved towards the kitchenette. Then, as he turned away for a moment, I slipped quickly back and round the corner of the passage beyond the stairhead. The cloakroom girl, duty done for the moment, had gone into the kitchen for a coffee as had her predecessor when Kitty and I had been there. I hurried past the first three doors, knowing they hid nothing of interest, and rounded the second corner. The door at the top of the short flight of steps stood open and I could hear Joanna's clear, ringing tones from the stage beyond. In the passage itself all was quiet. Softly, with wildly pumping heart, I started along it.

Another two doors opened with creaking hinges under my careful hands to display storerooms full of props; furniture stacked expertly on top of itself, boxes of books, vases and Victorian ornaments. By this time I was directly under the stage and the boards creaked as the actors moved about over my head. The passage had widened now into an open space, lit only by one naked electric light bulb. I wondered whether people often came down here and where would be the safest place to hide a prisoner where no sound he might make could be overheard.

Cautiously, my ears straining to the limits to detect instantly any slightest sound, I moved round the huge mounds of dust-covered furniture and great wicker baskets full of forgotten costumes. Hidden away at the far end was another short passage ending in a dark, grimy window. A faint glow coming from it indicated that it gave onto some basement area which had a street lamp just above it. And here, too, was another door, out of the way of the usual to-ing and fro-ing below the stage: an ideal hiding place.

Above me the Clown began to sing: "O mistress mine, where are you roaming?" You'd be surprised! I thought with a touch of grim humour. My hands were sticky with sweat and I wiped them down my skirt. Gently I took hold of the doorknob and slowly turned it. It resisted the pressure. Locked. There was no sound from within, but to my heightened senses the very silence held a listening quality. The door was thick and the cracks round its edges had been filled in with bulky draught-excluder. It must be virtually soundproof. I put my mouth against the lock and said clearly, "Is anyone there?" The words struck a grotesque echo in my mind of illicit séances in the common room at school. One thump for yes, two thumps for no.

My mouth to the crack again: "If you are there, you'll have to speak loudly, the door cracks are padded."

And at last, faintly but unmistakably, the reply I'd been waiting for. "Who is that?"

I ignored the question. "You are Etienne Lefevre?"

The voice rose excitedly, became more clearly audible. "Suzanne! *C'est toi?*"

"No, it's Ginnie Clements," I said, and had no time to wonder at the volte-face reversion to my right name. "Can you come nearer to the door? I can't hear you very well."

Incredibly there was a faint laugh. "*Hélas* no, mademoiselle, I regret. I am held to the bed."

My mind raced furiously. "How many people come into contact with you?"

"Only Stephen and his so disagreeable sister."

"Not Laurence?"

There was a slight pause. "*Non, pas* Laurence."

161

"At what times do they bring your food?"

"*Quoi?*"

"Your food—when do they bring it?"

"In the morning early, at midday and at about six hours, but I have no hunger. Mademoiselle, you will release me?"

"I intend to try. Do you ever come out of there?"

"*Mais oui.* When Stephen brings my breakfast and again late in the evening when the theatre is empty. He takes me to his dressing room to wash."

"There's no chance of breaking away from him?"

"He has a gun," Etienne said with devastating simplicity.

"A *gun?*" The implications of that were too wide to reflect on now and I pushed it out of my mind for the moment. My throat was aching with the strain of trying to shout quietly. "Have you any idea if there's more than one key?"

"*Je ne sais pas.*"

"And it's impossible for you to jump them when they bring the food?"

"Assuredly, or I should have done so. I am confined with steel."

"Steel?"

"A chain and lock."

"A padlock?"

"*C'est ça.*"

Above me and slightly to my right, the Clown broke into "Come away, come away, death." The second interval would not be long and the actors would be moving about more freely, might even slip down here for something. "I must go," I said quickly. "I shall try to think of a way to help you but it is dangerous for me to come again. Be patient and don't mention having spoken to me."

162

"Mademoiselle—Suzanne—does she know?"

"No, she doesn't. I'm going now. I'll do my best to get you out."

"*Merci,* mademoiselle. *A bientôt.* "

Step by step I retraced my way along the passage, past the danger point of the staircase and round the corner to the passage leading back to the public part of the theatre. My luck held. The girl was not at the cloakroom counter. I entered the foyer at the exact moment that the first members of the audience reached it from the opposite direction. My mind was spinning with wild surmises. It was almost unbelievable that I had at last managed to locate Etienne. At least he was all right so far; that was something. The next problem was to work out how to free him. Crazily I contemplated hiding under the stage until Stephen or Rachel came with his food and then—then what? Even if I could overpower Rachel, Etienne would be unable to help me, padlocked to the bed, and she might not have that key with her. He would only be released when Stephen was there to keep an eye on him. With his gun.

If only Suzanne were more stable she might prove an invaluable ally, but in her present state she was more likely to precipitate some crisis.

"Ginnie, I didn't see you! Hello!" It was Kitty at my side. "What are you doing here?"

"Oh, I just thought I'd pop in and see how things are going. You're not on duty again, are you?"

"I'm selling programs. It should have been Barbara, but she had a dental appointment this afternoon and her face is all swollen, so I said I'd come. Are you going to stay for a while?"

163

Marcus wasn't expecting me back till after ten. "Just for a few minutes. Are there any free seats?"

"Yes, one or two. I'll join you."

So it was that yet again I sat through the second half of *Twelfth Night* with Kitty beside me and my mind circling round the man imprisoned beneath the stage. All their efforts to frighten me away had failed and at last I had the answer to everything in my grasp.

"I hear Mrs. Davidson's back from holiday and you've finished at Culpepper's," Kitty whispered between scenes. "What are you going to do now?"

"I've got a job as secretary-receptionist at the George."

"Good for you. Any chance of a free meal?"

I smiled. "Not a hope."

"Coming to the end of play party on Saturday?"

"I hadn't thought of it," I said slowly. Of course, next week would be back to the rehearsal routine, which meant that as people would be in and out of the theatre all day, it would be that much more difficult to approach Etienne unnoticed. In any case now that I knew where he was, I was anxious to get him out as soon as possible. It was almost a month now since we had both arrived in Westhampton. I realized that Kitty was still whispering about the next production.

"What did you say they're doing?"

"Christopher Fry—*Venus Observed*. They're opening on the first of November. It's the last one before the Christmas presentations."

Christmas. I closed my mind to the prospect of spending it alone at the flat. The play wound its way to a close. I had stayed longer than I'd intended. "See you Saturday, then," Kitty said cheerfully.

"Perhaps."

The wind caught my coat and tore it apart, whistling coldly through the wool of my sweater. I shivered and hurried to the car, holding tightly onto the door as I opened it to prevent its being snatched out of my hand. Marcus's light was a very welcome sight as I turned into the Beeches and he was at the window watching out for my return.

I let myself into the flat and collected the night clothes and sponge bag I'd left ready before going out. His ring at the bell came just as I reached the hall again, and I opened the door.

"No problems?"

"No."

"Thank God. I might tell you this has got me thoroughly jittery. I've been pacing up and down all evening, wondering what you were doing and if there were any sinister figures looming up around you."

"Poor Marcus. Never mind, I don't think it will be going on much longer."

"You said that before. Do you mean you're leaving?"

"I—don't know."

"It depends on Carl, no doubt," he said heavily. He gave me a crooked smile. "All right, I can't say you didn't warn me. Come on, I'll see you safely into the flat. Have you got the car keys?"

I handed them to him.

"Turn out the hall light. We don't want anyone to see the switch." I did so and together we went across the short stretch of gravel which separated our front doors, keeping

165

close into the angle of the house. He opened his door for me and stood aside to let me pass.

"Good night, Marcus, and thank you for looking after me so well."

"Don't mention it. I'm only sorry it's a temporary arrangement. Good night, Ginnie; sleep well."

A moment later I was alone in the warm little hall. Outside the engine of my car started up and moved away in the direction of the garage. With a sigh which I didn't stop to define I moved towards the stairs.

Chapter 12

THE next few days passed uneventfully. I was kept fairly busy at the George, but every free moment my brain was worrying at the problem of how to effect Etienne's release and I seemed to be getting no nearer a solution. It was the gun I came up against each time, but I was not completely convinced of its veracity. To someone with Etienne's background, it would no doubt seem quite natural that an actor in a small provincial theatre should possess firearms. For my own part, I doubted it. It was much more likely to be a stage prop. The point was whether I was convinced enough of my theory to risk putting it to the test.

Marcus and I had slipped easily enough into our nightly switch of flats and the knowledge of being able to count on an undisturbed sleep was incredibly comforting. He had reported another telephone call in the night watches but no more imminent dangers. Yet time was passing relentlessly. It was three days now since I'd held my whispered consultation with Etienne. He would be wondering whether after all I was to be any help to him.

On the Friday morning, Kitty phoned me at the George. "Ginnie, we always turn to you in an emergency! Could you possibly help out at the theatre this evening? Barbara's face is still bad—apparently she's developed an abscess, poor thing, and now one of the girls in the kitchen can't make it. I wouldn't ask you again, except that you seem quite to enjoy dropping in there."

My brain clicked into action. "Yes, all right. The only problem is that I can't make it between six-thirty and seven-thirty. I could go straight from work, though, and set out all the cups and things. That would make it easier for whoever's left to cope with the pre-show coffee." And Etienne received his evening meal about six.

"That would be a help, yes. The intervals are the main panic."

"The only thing is—" I tried to keep the excitement out of my voice. "How will I get into the theatre at that time? Will anyone be there?"

"You can always get the key from old Bert, the caretaker. He lives in a flat over the mews, just opposite the entrance. I'll give him a ring and tell him to expect you. Then there'll be no problem."

"Thanks." My hand was shaking as I put the receiver down.

Marcus came into the bar as usual at lunchtime, and I was able to slip across and tell him it would be after ten again that evening before I would be back at the Beeches.

He eyed me shrewdly. "Things are hotting up, aren't they?"

"It's beginning to look like it."

168

"Promise me you won't take any chances."

"No more than I have to," I answered evasively, and he had to be content with that. I drove to the theatre straight after work and duly called on "old Bert."

"I'm sorry to disturb you," I said brightly, taking the key he had ready for me. "I suppose you're used to it, though. Is this the only key there is?"

"Mr. Grey has one to the stage door, o' course, and I think there's a spare up in the office at the theatre, but this here's mine and you're welcome to borrow it any time, long as you let me have it back safe."

I thanked him, as much for the information as his offer and for the first time myself unlocked the door at the foot of the stairs and pulled it shut behind me. Rachel would doubtless let herself in by the stage door, either with Laurence's key or the spare, but I had no wish to warn her of my presence by leaving this door open. I ran lightly up the stairs and straight along the passage. It was just after five-thirty. Etienne's door was still firmly locked. I bent to the keyhole. "Etienne?"

"*Ello?*"

"Are you still chained to the bed?"

"*Bien sûr.* What is happening? Each day I hope—"

"I know. I'm going to hide out here and see just what the procedure is when they bring your food. I've a pair of pliers in my bag and if there's any chance at all of taking her by surprise I should be able to cut through the chains. But I really intend only to watch today. I'd rather have Suzanne or someone with me when it comes to getting you out of here. I'm going now. Rachel should be here soon."

169

I eased myself carefully between two anonymous mounds of furniture shrouded in filthy dust sheets, and prepared to wait for Rachel. The minutes passed, punctuated by the ticking of my watch, loud as a time bomb in the stillness. Then at last, somewhere up above me, I heard a door close and footsteps approaching. A moment later the light bulb flared into lurid life and I forced my head down between my knees. I had reckoned that from where I was I should be able to see diagonally into the room where Etienne lay.

Rachel was coming down the short flight of steps just along the passage. Moments later she passed within inches of me. There was a click as the key turned in the lock, the door opened and she went inside. Cautiously I raised my head. She was alone, but she was taking no chances. I saw with grudging admiration the method they had devised to keep their distance from their prisoner. An old trolley was just inside the room and it was on this that she unpacked the hot food she had brought wrapped in foil. I could hear the low murmur of her voice—Rachel never spoke loudly—but the words were indistinguishable. Nor, except for an outline on the bed, could I see Etienne Lefevre. When the food was set out, she pushed the trolley carefully over the floor towards the bed and he caught hold of it. I had only just time to duck down again before Rachel appeared in the doorway with a tray of dirty plates, no doubt Etienne's lunch dishes. Seconds later the door was shut and locked and her footsteps were retreating in the distance. The light clicked off, leaving small yellow discs floating in the darkness in front of my blinded eyes.

I stood up slowly, easing my cramped limbs and straight-

170

ening my dress. "Etienne," I called softly through the door, "I'll come back as soon as I can. *Bon appétit!*" I heard his low laugh in acknowledgment and then, with another glance at my watch, hurried back along the passage. My mind was so full of plans that I had pushed open the kitchen door before, too late, I realized that the light was already on and Rachel, stark panic on her face, had turned swiftly from the sink where she was washing Etienne's dirty plates. For a timeless moment we stared across the room at each other. She was the first to find her voice.

"What the devil are you doing here?"

I drew a steadying breath. "I might ask you the same thing." Was my expression as undeniably guilty as hers?

She said rapidly, "I brought along Stephen's costume which I'd washed and ironed." Her eyes flicked to the soapy plate still in her hand. "I found these in his dressing room. He probably had a snack here at lunchtime. They've already started preliminary rehearsals for the next show." She paused and, confidence returning, demanded accusingly, "How did you get in?"

"I borrowed the caretaker's key. Kitty arranged it." Thankfully I knew that could all be checked.

"I didn't notice the door open."

"I probably pulled it to after me. I've come to set out the cups for the early coffee. I'm helping tonight but I can't get here before seven-thirty."

She stared at me without speaking and I knew she was trying to assess the truth of what I said and at the same time to discover whether or not I had believed her quite plausible lie. It took quite an effort to break away from her gaze and start with trembling fingers to lay out the cups and saucers, fill the kettle and urn and pour the milk into the pan. I didn't look in her direction again, and after a moment I heard her turn back to the sink and go on with the dishes.

"Did Miss Davidson have a good holiday?" I asked casually, when I felt able to control my voice. I thought she was not going to reply, but after a moment she said briefly, "God knows." I didn't attempt any further conversation. When I had finished my self-allotted task, I meekly said goodbye and left her. I locked the door behind me, since she would let herself out the same way she had come in, and returned the key to Bert. Suppose it occurred to her to check what time I'd arrived at the theatre? Would Bert have registered it? He had only to mention a time some fifteen minutes before Rachel and I had come face to face in the kitchen for all her dormant suspicions to rise again like a swarm of hornets. I did not care to contemplate what she and Stephen might do then.

As soon as I reached the Beeches, I went and rang Marcus's bell. He took a quick look at my flushed face and pulled me into the hallway. "What's happened?"

"I was wondering if you'd like to come and see *Twelfth Night* this evening," I said jerkily.

"Of course I'll come, but why particularly this evening? You wouldn't let me go with you before."

"I think I'd feel safer if you were there. There are some rather dark alleyways to negotiate to get back to the car."

"And that's all the explanation you'll give me?"

"I'm afraid so, for the moment."

He sighed. "What time do you want to go?"

172

"About seven-thirty. I'm on duty and I said I couldn't get there earlier. I needed an excuse to be there around six—"

"And someone saw you." It was more statement than question.

"Yes."

"Then you finally admit that you're in danger?"

"I might be," I conceded.

"And I'm to be there as a kind of general insurance without having the slightest idea which direction the danger might come from?"

"I'm sorry, Marcus," I said helplessly, "I know I've no right to ask you—"

"On the contrary," he broke in brusquely, "as you well know, you've every right. It's just this continual lack of trust that rankles. However, I suppose you must play it your own way. I'll collect you just before seven-thirty and you can give me the rest of my sealed orders then."

We arrived at the theatre as the last bell was sounding in the foyer. There was no difficulty in Marcus's obtaining a single seat and I left him to join the girl on duty in the kitchen.

During the first act Stephen came to the kitchen, ostensibly to borrow some milk for the coffee backstage. "Well, well, Mrs. Clements! We meet again! I sometimes wonder if it wouldn't be simpler for you to take lodgings here."

I met his eye squarely. "Why, do you take in lodgers?"

A tremor crossed his face but he recovered quickly and gave a short laugh. "We could always make an exception, I suppose. Sister Rachel tells me you are no longer working partners."

173

"I was only engaged by Culpepper's for three weeks." Out of the corner of my eye I could see my fellow helper gazing at Stephen with silent adoration. Admittedly he was a handsome figure in doublet and hose; she could hardly be blamed for not appreciating that he might also be dangerous.

"And have you found other gainful employment?"

"Yes, I'm working at the George," I answered crisply, "and if I may say so, you'd better be getting backstage or you'll miss your entrance at the beginning of Act Two."

He smiled. "Dear Ginnie, you know the play better than I do, don't you? All right, I'll go. No doubt we'll meet again." Was there a threat hidden beneath that smile? A little chill touched me, raising the hairs on the back of my neck.

"He's gorgeous, isn't he?" Linda said with a sigh. "I could listen to him talk all day!"

It was undeniably an attractive voice. I remembered the first words I had heard it say: "He never knew what hit him."

There were other faces I knew beside Marcus's among the coffee queue that evening. Moira Francis and the boys were there. "Hello, Miss Durrell! The Beeches is well represented tonight—we've just seen Mr. Sinclair. I didn't know this was one of your hobbies!"

I smiled steadily, filling their cups. "I've always loved anything to do with the theatre. Are you enjoying the play?"

"Oh, very much. Roger's doing it for O-levels, but it's a sheer treat for me. Viola's excellent, isn't she?"

They moved away and a little later Marcus took his turn. "All well?" he asked in a low voice.

"So far, so good."

"I'll wait for you at the foot of the stairs after the show."

174

The bells sounded, the cups were collected, washed and set out ready for the next interval. Perhaps it had been unwise to challenge Stephen about lodgers; he might take it as proof that I knew something. I was very thankful to know that I had Marcus's company on the way home.

I'm not sure at what stage I reached my decision, but it was all fully resolved by the time that Marcus pulled my hand through his arm and hurried me along the poorly lighted alleyway to his car. I settled back against the cushions with a sigh of relief. It seemed to have been going on forever, this fearful hurrying from the theatre to the car and the almost tangible sense of relief when I reached it in safety. All at once I felt that I could bear it no longer.

"By the way," Marcus remarked as he started up the engine, "I'm almost sure I've identified my assailant of the other night."

I looked at him quickly. "Stephen Darby?"

"So you knew all the time."

"I suspected. Marcus, I have to go to London tomorrow. I'm not sure what time I'll get back."

The car swerved fractionally. "To see Carl?"

"Yes. I have no choice now but to tell him the whole story. I need his help."

"Mine is not enough?" There was a touch of bitterness in his voice.

"It's not that," I said gently, "but you see he knows ninety percent of it already. I only have to fill in the details. He'll know what should be done."

"When will you go?"

"In the morning. I have the weekend free of the George.

175

The trouble is I might not be able to contact Carl straight-away. I doubt if he'll be spending much time alone at the flat. It might be evening before I can track him down."

"In other words," Marcus said unevenly, "you'll be away overnight."

"It's possible. I'll take some things in case I need them. There's a hotel just round the corner from the flat. I'll book there."

He made no comment and a moment later we turned off Grove Street into the square. Silently he waited while I collected my night things and came with me to his own door.

"Thank you for coming with me tonight."

"A pleasure," he said briefly.

I hesitated. "Marcus, don't look like that. It'll be all right."

He moved restlessly. "I'm probably being melodramatic, but I have a feeling this is really goodbye."

"But I should be back tomorrow—Sunday at the latest."

"Perhaps. I'll probably sleep at your flat anyway, to keep an eye on things. Also, if they should phone they'll think you're still there if I pick up the receiver."

"I'll ring and let you know when to expect me."

"All right. I hope things work out the way you want them." He bent down suddenly and brushed his lips against mine. Then he gave me a little push into the hall and closed the door from the outside. Slowly, buffeted with conflicting emotions, I went up the stairs into the warmly welcoming flat.

By ten o'clock the next morning I was driving back along the road where, four long weeks ago, Etienne Lefevre had

176

bumped into my car and started the whole thing rolling. It was one o'clock as I crossed Chelsea Bridge and turned along the embankment. I had intended to go straight to the Kingston Hotel for lunch, but instead I found myself turning into the familiar forecourt of the block of luxury flats which had been home to me until the last month. I still had the key in my bag but I had no intention of using it.

There was no sign of the porter; he was probably at lunch. I took the lift up to the third floor and walked along the thickly carpeted corridor to the square landing outside Number 5. With a feeling of sick expectancy I rang the bell. I think I knew immediately that no one was home. There's a certain quality attached to the sound of a doorbell ringing in an empty house. Nevertheless I waited for a few minutes before disconsolately retracing my steps to the lift. There was no way of knowing where Carl now spent his Saturdays. He might even be away for the weekend. The sudden thought brought panic in its wake. I knew that I would not dare to return to Westhampton without seeing him.

All I could do was wait. I drove round the corner, booked a room at the Kingston in the name of Miss Durrell, left my case in it and forced myself to eat some lunch.

During the afternoon, which I spent wandering up and down the King's Road, I phoned the flat at roughly hourly intervals. I had decided that if Carl should answer, I would hang up without speaking and go straight round to the flat. The eventuality did not arise. By five o'clock it was obvious that I should indeed be spending the night in London. If he hadn't returned to the flat by bedtime, I should have to wait till Sunday evening, when he would surely come home.

At six o'clock, back in the small hotel room, I phoned Marcus to report my lack of progress and intention of remaining overnight. I felt curiously disembodied, poised between two different worlds, and it was a comfort to hear his voice. I went down to dinner and pushed some food round and round my plate. Surely Carl would be home the next time I tried to phone. But he wasn't. I went back upstairs, lay on the bed and tried to concentrate on the television. At the Little Theatre, preparations would be under way for the party after the show. I wondered if Suzanne would be there.

Eight o'clock, nine o'clock, ten. And still the telephone shrilled unanswered at Berkley Court. At last, unable to bear the confines of the room any longer, I caught up my coat and bag and went out to the car. I drove round the corner and along the road to the flats, turned into the courtyard and parked right at the far end. By counting the number of windows from the end of the building, I could work out which was the sitting-room window of our own flat. It was still in darkness. I wrapped my coat about me, turned up the collar and settled back to listen to the car radio. I resolved to stay where I was until midnight. After that I would give up and go back to the hotel.

They came just before eleven. I jerked upright as the giant headlamps raked carelessly over the huddled shapes of the parked cars and two Bentleys slid simultaneously to a halt in the position Carl always used. I felt cold and sick. I had counted on his returning alone. It would be impossible to speak to him if he was with, say, Leonie Pratt. A laughing, noisy crowd had now spilled out of both cars and moved in a body towards the lighted doorway. I could make out Carl's

178

tall figure, and the short, dumpy shape of Greg Baxter. The others I wasn't sure about from this distance. I went on staring mindlessly after them long after the last one disappeared into the warm hallway. Now what? Should I after all return to the hotel and come back in the morning? There was no point in waiting for the crowd to go, it could well be two or three o'clock.

Light blossomed in the long windows I had pinpointed. I sat numbly staring up at them, watching the occasional splash of colour pass behind the glass. How well I knew those ghastly parties; how I had hated them.

Time crawled by. A voice on the radio said, "The time is eleven-thirty. Here are the news headlines." I leaned forward and switched it off and in the same instant made up my mind. If I went back to the hotel now, keyed up as I was to speak to Carl, I stood no chance of sleep. Nor had I any intention of shivering out here any longer like an outcast. Before I could change my mind, I got out and locked the car, wrapped my coat tightly about me and set off across the forecourt.

The hall was warm, soothing to my wind-chilled face. A porter I didn't know looked up from the desk. "Mr. Clements," I said, and added quickly, "It's all right; he's expecting me." He nodded, knowing of the crowd already upstairs, and I made my way unchallenged to the lift and the third floor. I could hear the music as I walked along the corridor. It was a source of never-ending wonder to me that no one ever complained. Perhaps no one slept in this place before two o'clock in the morning.

I stopped at the smoothly polished door and put my finger firmly on the bell.

Chapter 13

IT was Buntie Maynard who opened the door, glass in one hand, cigarette holder in the other. For a moment she gazed at me almost without recognition, then she gave a little shriek and called over her shoulder, "Carl! Come and see who we've got here!"

They all came crowding out of the sitting room, exclaiming and laughing, their faces flushed and voices shrill. My eyes went past them to Carl, rigid against the door frame. With an effort he pushed himself away from it and the crowd parted before him. I kept my eyes desperately on his, closing my mind to the babbling crowd around us, and some message must have got across because his gaze, hard and cold as blue ice, altered slightly. I said drily, "I'm sorry to interrupt but I have to speak to you."

"Get Ginnie a drink, someone!" Jessie Winthrop called, and added with a giggle, "Sorry, I'm treating you like a guest in your own home!"

There was a small, splintered silence as all of them wondered whether it was indeed still my home. I smiled tightly and allowed Carl to take my arm and lead me into the sitting room, thrumming and vibrating with the music on the stereo. No soft piano concertos here, I thought bleakly, and closed my mind to the comparison. Buntie, slightly more drunk than the others, was accordingly less cautious. "Darling, where on earth have you been all this time? Carl was like a clam; he would never tell us a thing!"

I took the glass Robert Winthrop handed me, but before I could reply, Carl said steadily, "There's no mystery. She's been down at Westhampton. We've seen each other several times."

Buntie gave him a playful pat. "Naughty boy! And all the time we thought you didn't know where she was and were trying to console you!"

I thought in a panic, if she doesn't stop I shall burst into tears. And again Carl came unexpectedly to the rescue. "Look, everyone, Ginnie and I have some things we need to discuss. Would you mind if we postponed this get-together till next weekend?"

There was a general, slightly embarrassed chorus of assent and everyone began to make for the door. Above the elaborate ritual of apologies and extravagant thanks, I caught Buntie's wail: "But darling Ginnie's only just arrived! Aren't we even to be allowed to talk to her?"

Despite the almost oppressive heat in the room, I found I was shivering and set the cold glass carefully down on one of the little lacquered tables. Looking round the beautiful room, I now acknowledged for the first time that I had never liked it. I felt far more at home at the Beeches after four weeks than I had here after four years. It was all so pretentious somehow and self-conscious, like a stage set that would be greeted by a spontaneous burst of applause when the curtain went up. And here Carl and I had lived our stilted and artificial life together, as though an unseen spotlight followed our every move. The result of it, as I now saw, was that we didn't know each other at all.

The outer door closed at last. Carl came into the room and switched off the compulsive beating and pounding of the record. Silence leaped upon us, assaulting our eardrums almost as painfully as had the intense noise of a moment before. I reached quickly for the glass. He was still standing by the far wall, looking across at me.

"I'm sorry I broke up your party," I began shakily.

"It wasn't my idea, I assure you. Having decided I mustn't be alone, they insist on coming back with me nearly every evening. No doubt they mean well, but I wish to God they wouldn't."

"I'm also sorry it's so late. I did try to get you earlier but there was no reply."

"We've been at the theatre all day—preliminary discussions, casting, auditions, you know the routine." There was a short silence. Carl said abruptly, "How's your drink?"

"All right, thanks." It struck me for the first time that out of them all he had been the only one who was completely sober. I had planned several alternative opening remarks for this moment but now that I needed them they faded from my mind, leaving it blank. Over by the door Carl waited. At last I said in desperation, "I need your help."

"Oh?" His eyes were watchful and wary. My hands tightened on the glass and keeping my eyes on it, I said rapidly, "It's about Etienne Lefevre. I know where he is."

Another silence. Then he said tonelessly, "Didn't you always?"

I shook my head. "I'd no idea what was going on."

He moved impatiently. "Oh, come on, Ginnie, you'll have to do better than that. That evening in Westhampton—"

"I tell you I didn't know. I just—threw out Madame's name to see if it would have the same effect on you as it had on the others."

"And did it?"

I said numbly, "You know the answer to that."

"But if you really didn't know anything, why didn't you explain? Why let me go on thinking—"

"You weren't in the mood for explanations and nor was I. It was easier just to let you go."

"I see."

I looked up quickly. "I didn't mean—I only meant—"

He walked unhurriedly across the room and sat down on the sofa beside me. "Look, Ginnie, we've the hell of a lot to talk about, but let's leave the personal side until we've cleared up the rest. You'd better start from the beginning."

Stumblingly, with him prompting me from time to time, I gave him the rough outline of what had happened from the moment Etienne's Fiat had sent me spinning into the ditch outside Westhampton to my whispered consultation with him at the theatre the day before. When I had finished, Carl said slowly, "So it really was a genuine kidnapping after all. We were never convinced of that. What first gave you the impression they were suspicious of you?"

183

"I think Stephen was all along. I'm not sure why, but after a while there were phone calls and doorbells ringing in the middle of the night and someone always watching me from a seat in the park."

He stared at me incredulously. "And you still went on with it? Were you out of your mind? Why in God's name didn't you come to me before?" And then, without waiting for a reply, he added sharply, "No one actually tried to harm you physically, did they?"

"No, the worst time was probably when someone climbed up on my balcony one night. I think it was Stephen."

"What happened?"

"Marcus went after him."

He moved fractionally. "Ah yes, Marcus. He was—with you?"

"Actually I was with him. I'd gone for dinner at his flat. He—happened to look out of the window and saw the figure."

"I see. Then I suppose I have to be grateful to him. How much does he know about it?"

"Nothing; I didn't dare tell him."

Although I didn't turn my head, I knew Carl was watching me intently, but all he said, after a pause, was, "I suppose I'd better tell you my side of it, though you know most of it from what Suzanne Grey told you. The first I knew was when Madame rang me in great distress a few days after—after you'd left and asked me to go straight round. She told me everything then, that the change we'd all noticed in her a few months previously had been caused not by her son's death but by his sudden and unwelcome arrival in London.

184

I gather life had become a nightmare for her. Not only was she terrified of being discovered harbouring a criminal, and an illegal entrant at that, but from what she said I think he used to knock her about a bit to try to get more money out of her. She daren't invite anyone to the house and she was frightened every time the doorbell rang. Added to all this, he would regularly disappear for days at a time. She never knew where he went but she was convinced he had established contact with some dope ring and was back in the old routine. He'd always been very vague about how he managed to get into this country, and she was only able to fill in the gaps when Suzanne went to see her. By that time she was nearly out of her mind with worry because the police had phoned to report finding the Fiat, which, of course, was registered in her name. It had apparently been parked without lights on the embankment."

"Stephen must have driven it back when he came to post the ransom note. I presume that had a London postmark?"

"Yes. Anyway, Suzanne's news about his contact with the theatre was the first real lead, and of course since they'd helped him before, the obvious assumption was that they were helping him again; in other words that they were concealing him at his own request as a means of extortion. It was easy to explain away Suzanne's ignorance of what had happened. She was so highly strung she could easily have made a slip and given everything away."

"So your first visit to Westhampton was purely reconnaissance?"

"Exactly, and in the meantime we had decided to ignore the ransom note. They knew Madame would never go to the

185

police with it, since that would mean exposing Etienne's presence here. We concluded it was simply a question of letting them pay for his keep instead of Madame, which seemed an admirable arrangement." He paused. "You can imagine I was somewhat surprised to find you there."

"And you tried to warn me to keep away from the theatre."

"In rather a clumsy way, yes, though it never occurred to me for a moment that you were in actual danger. And then, when you suddenly came out with Madame's name—well, I just wasn't thinking straight at all. I wanted to believe you were in on the plan but I never managed to convince myself and I never mentioned your being there to Madame."

"So, what happens next?" I asked after a moment.

"I suppose we'll have to get him away from them, though Lord knows what we'll do with him then. No doubt his poor mother will be lumbered again. One thing's certain, I'm damned if I'm going to risk my civil liberty or whatever by being an accessory after the fact. Is that the right phrase? It sounds good, anyway. If we go to the police it'll come out that Madame was sheltering him before the kidnapping though I imagine there'll be extenuating circumstances."

"Perhaps we should leave it to her to decide. We'll have to tell her, anyway, that I've located him."

"Yes, but I imagine the best thing would be for us to drive down tomorrow and force a confrontation of some kind. We'll have to play it by ear when the time comes." He stood up and took his own glass and mine over to the bar. "Which leaves us free to turn to more personal problems." I sat unmoving, listening to the splash of the liquid and Carl's

186

footsteps coming back over the carpet. "You know," he said conversationally, handing me my glass, "when I saw you just now standing at the door, I thought you'd come to ask for a divorce." The lengthening silence jarred on my taut nerves. "Do you want one, Ginnie?"

I looked up and met the force of his eyes. "Do you?" I countered.

"Like hell." He sat down carefully, his eyes on the level of the brimming glass. "That Marcus chap, though. I presume he is in love with you?"

"It's possible," I said faintly.

"He's obviously much more your type than I am."

"Undoubtedly. There's one snag, though."

"Which is?"

"That I'm fool enough still to love you."

He reached out and gripped my hand tightly. "Fool's right. Ginnie, you know sackcloth and ashes were never my scene, but for what it's worth, I'm sorry about Leonie. Will that do?"

I smiled tremulously. "For one who in his time has spoken all the most lyrical love words in the English language, you don't cut a very romantic figure, my darling."

"I do love you, though, in my own selfish, inconsiderate way. One hell of a lot. That's been borne in on me in no uncertain way these last few weeks. When you went away it was—like an amputation." He turned to look at me, still gripping my hand. "I want you back, make no mistake about that, but I'm not fool enough to ask you to come back to the kind of life we had before. We wouldn't stand any more chance of making a go of it than we did last time. I've been trying to see a way round the problem and I think I've found it." With his free hand he reached for his glass and drank. I sat unmoving. "Have you read anything about the new art centre they're building up in the North Riding? It's to be a fantastic project—theatre, library, art gallery all in one complex. They were looking for people to run it and I put my name forward. I heard the other day I've been accepted, but the final decision is up to you."

"You mean you'd leave London?"

"I'd come down from time to time, of course, to act or produce, and we could take a furnished flat for as long as we needed one, but half the trouble has been that I've been far too bogged down in the glamour and prestige of life here; you know that better than anyone. We'd be off to a much better start working together on this new challenge—and I do mean together, because I should need your help. So what do you say? Will you come to Yorkshire with me and make it all worthwhile?"

For the first time I saw in his face the uncertainty, the basic insecurity he had admitted but which I'd never been able to accept. "Yes, darling," I said softly, "I'll come."

Chapter 14

I WOKE the next morning to find Carl propped on one elbow looking down on me. "I'm still trying to convince myself that it isn't all a dream, but since you seem real enough perhaps we'd better think about getting some breakfast."

I stretched sleepily. "What time is it?"

"Just after nine. I'll wait till half past and then give Madame a ring and let her know we're coming round."

The sun was shining when we left the flat an hour or so later. "I've brought a few things just in case I need them," Carl said, tossing a small grip onto the back seat of the Bentley, "but we should be back tonight if all goes well." A tiny pinprick appeared in my bubble of happiness. If all goes well. We still had a difficult and perhaps dangerous task ahead of us before we could relax and begin our new life together.

We collected my own case from the Kingston and Carl paid the bill; I had at least made some use of the room during the long hours of waiting yesterday. Then we drove through the russet and gold of Regent's Park to Madame Lefevre's beautiful home. She met us at the door and, despite her anxiety, swept me immediately into a warm embrace. "It is so good to see you again, *chérie*. Carl has been *distrait* without you."

"Thank you," I said humbly and followed her into the vast first-floor drawing room overlooking the park. She was a charming woman, rather plump now and in her late sixties but still with the unassailable chic of the true Frenchwoman.

"Eh bien," she said, when the pert little maid had brought in a tray of coffee. "Tell me about Etienne."

So once again I went through the outlines of the story, of how I had first heard of the kidnapping and how it was through Suzanne that I too had learned of the victim's identity.

"I hope you will forgive a foolish old woman her pride," Madame said ruefully, passing me a delicate bone china cup and saucer. "I could not bring myself to tell even my closest friends of the true position."

"Of course we understand," I said gently.

"And now of course we must go to his assistance." Her eyes clouded and I knew achingly that she was preparing, because she would admit of no choice, to go back to a life of uncertainty and intermittent assault with Etienne concealed once more on the premises. And I thought how hard it was to equate the different parts that made up this man: the ruthless drug pusher, Suzanne's passionate lover, the laughing voice that had spoken to me through the locked door and the heartless, bullying son.

Carl said quietly, "Will it be possible for us to get into the

190

theatre, Ginnie? Surely it will be locked up, being Sunday?"

"Yes, they have a day's break after the last night of a production before they really get under way with rehearsals for the next one. However, the caretaker has a key and he knows me."

He glanced at his watch. "What time did you say Rachel takes his meals?"

"About midday and again at six."

"It's eleven now. We haven't a hope of being there for his lunch, which means we must wait for the evening meal. I've a pair of wire cutters in the boot, so if she hasn't got the padlock key with her we should still be able to free him quite easily. I've a torch as well. I can't think of anything else we might need."

I shivered involuntarily and Carl's hand closed over mine. "Hang on, darling; it's nearly over now."

Madame said worriedly, "I do not like to think of you putting yourselves in danger for my son. Perhaps after all the police—"

"No," I said quickly, "it's better this way. Try not to worry."

She said in a low voice, "If only he would return to France—"

"We'll certainly suggest it," Carl said grimly. "After all this trouble, I feel it's the least he can do."

She shrugged expressively. I leaned forward and replaced my cup and saucer on the tray, and Carl got to his feet. "We might as well be on our way." He took her small plump hands in his. *"Soyez tranquille, madame, tout sera bien."*

Her lips trembled as she reached up to kiss his cheek. "I shall pray for you," she said simply.

Then we were in the car again and following the route I

191

had taken so haphazardly four weeks earlier. There were quite a lot of cars about on this cold, sunny Sunday morning, but the holiday traffic of my earlier journey was past.

"In a way I'll be quite sorry to leave Westhampton," I said reflectively. "I've made some good friends there."

"Yes, I suppose so. Oh, by the way, they told me at the Kingston there was a telephone call for you this morning, a Mr. Sinclair. He didn't leave a message. I presume that would be Marcus?"

"Yes."

Carl's eyes were on the road, narrowed against the sunshine. "Was there ever any point when you felt you might be able to—reciprocate his feelings?"

"Not really. He said himself it was a pity I was so hung-up on my husband."

"Bless you for staying 'hung-up,' " Carl said quietly, "and don't grieve too much for Westhampton. From what I hear, Roydstone Park sounds a similar kind of town."

"How soon will we be moving?"

"Not until the spring, and of course *Richard* is looming in the meantime, but we can go up at weekends and get the feel of the place, perhaps start house-hunting. Once we get settled there I hope to do more television work, too. Yorkshire Television have approached me several times but I've been too involved down here to be able to accept anything. Though of course, it's the theatre up there which I'll be mainly concerned with. Just think of it, a theatre where we'll have a more or less free hand! In time we can build up a touring company, too. There's just no limit to the scope which will open up."

"Carl, I've been thinking. I'm afraid I'll have to stay in Westhampton at least for this week. For one thing I'm working at the George and they're entitled to a week's notice. They're very short-handed at the moment. Then there's the flat. I'll have to arrange to sublet it or something. Mr. Henry will probably be able to help. And there are so many people I couldn't possibly miss saying goodbye to."

"Far be it from me to try to deflect you from your principles, my love! I might not manage the whole week with you, but I'll stay as long as I can. Robert Harling is one of the reasons I ought to get back; he'll be signing in for rehearsals shortly. Let's hope none of this will reverberate on him. I'd be most loth to see my brand-new Clarence in clink! We've not far to go now. Will we be in time for lunch at the George? It would save you having to start cooking the minute we reach the flat."

"We should be; they go on serving it till two. This is the spot where Etienne bumped into me, by the way."

It was five minutes short of two as we drew up outside the George and hurried inside. Jane raised a hand as we passed the desk. We went straight through to the dining room but neither of us did full justice to the traditional Sunday lunch of roast beef. Now that we were back at the centre of the unresolved business which awaited completion, I was becoming more and more apprehensive of what lay ahead.

After the meal Carl went with me to Mrs. Baillie's room to hand in my notice. She expressed conventional regrets, but I was amused to see that she was far more interested in Carl, waiting patiently in the background.

"By the way, darling," I said over my shoulder, "Mrs.

193

Baillie would be undyingly grateful if you'd address a meeting of her Townswomen's Guild." I smiled into her startled, slightly embarrassed eyes. "And I might as well confess, Mrs. Baillie, that Carl is my husband."

"Really?" Her face broke into a delighted smile and her eyes dropped to the ring on my finger which Carl had firmly replaced the night before. "I did realize, of course, that you were married, but I must admit I never for one moment—" She broke off in confusion and we all laughed.

"I should be delighted to address your meeting, Mrs. Baillie," Carl said easily, with the smooth charm which had enslaved so many, and we promised to fix a date before we left Westhampton.

By the time we had stopped the car outside the Beeches, Marcus was standing waiting for us. I went over to him, followed more slowly by Carl.

"Looking at your face," Marcus said crisply, "I don't have to ask how things are. I phoned you at the hotel this morning but of course you weren't there. I can't say I was very surprised." "I have a feeling this is really goodbye," he had said.

Carl had reached us now, and held out his hand. After a second's hesitation, Marcus took it. "I want to thank you very sincerely for your kindness to Ginnie," Carl said quietly. "Your support has been a great comfort to her."

I saw a muscle twitch in Marcus's temple and held my breath. "I'm glad of that," he replied after a moment.

Carl smiled slightly. "And to answer your unspoken comment, I intend to take much better care of her myself in future."

Marcus smiled and relaxed a little. "I'm delighted to hear

194

it. Here's your key, Ginnie. I hope you explained the extreme propriety of our little arrangement, since I need to collect my pyjamas!"

"Oh, I did. Come in for a moment, anyway." The emerald green carpet was back in place, as good as new.

"I collected it yesterday," Marcus said, catching my delighted exclamation.

"Bless you, and you've laid it beautifully. We must settle up with you. I bet it was expensive." I added to Carl, "I left the washing machine on one day and nearly flooded the place!"

He was looking about him with evident approval. "I haven't been allowed in here before. It's most attractive."

"Look at this," I said proudly, opening the drawing-room door. The browns and golds of furniture and brocade lay bathed in the rich light of the afternoon sun.

"Perfect! We must have a room like this in Yorkshire!" He told Marcus of the proposed move and we all talked together for a few minutes. Then Marcus said a little diffidently, "There's one thing I have to ask. Is all the—danger over now?"

Carl glanced across at me. "Not quite."

"Is there anything at all I can do?"

"I think we at least owe him a full explanation, don't you, Ginnie?" I nodded and as briefly as possible Carl sketched in the details. Marcus of course already knew of the Picardy Hotel, the watchers in the park and the theatre connection. I saw him nod slowly as the last points fell neatly into place.

"I'd better go along with you this evening," he said quietly.

Carl hesitated. "We've no right to expect that."

"You didn't expect it. Of course, the best thing would be for Ginnie to remain safely here, but I know she'd never agree to that."

"I certainly wouldn't. In any case, Bert wouldn't give you the key, nor would you know how to find the right room once you got inside."

"If you mean it, Marcus, I'd be very grateful for you to come along. We might well need all the help we can get."

"Fine. What time will you be leaving here?"

"About five-thirty—in an hour and a half."

"Right, I'll come back then."

By the time he returned I had changed into a dark sweater and trews, which I felt would merge with the shadows under the stage. With dry mouth and painfully beating heart I followed the other two out of the flat and pulled the door shut behind me. There was no turning back now. The sunset was fading from the sky as we drove through the quiet streets and the first lamps were coming on. "Only another fortnight till summertime ends," Marcus remarked. For what was probably the last time, we drew up in my usual parking place and locked the car. If luck was with us, we should be back here in about half an hour with Etienne safely beside us. Through the alleyway, ghostly in the twilight, we went and out into Phoenix Street. Beyond the lamp at the corner, the cobbled mews lay in shadows, its windows giving back the last lurid glow in the sky. With Marcus and Carl at my side, I knocked on the door of Bert's flat and he came to answer it in slippered feet.

"Ah, 'tis you, Miss Durrell. Would you be wanting the key again?"

"Please, Bert. I'll drop it through your letterbox when we've finished with it." He nodded and touched his forehead to the two men in a quaintly old-world gesture. Silently we walked across to the door. Carl unlocked it and we followed him in and pulled it gently shut again. My heart was beating high in my throat now, ears straining for any sound which might indicate Rachel was there before us. There was none.

Carl switched on the torch and with his hand gripping mine we went up the steep stairs and along the tunnel of its light down the dark passage, Marcus right behind us. Never before had I been so painfully aware of the creaking boards beneath our feet. Three people undeniably made three times as much noise, however softly they moved. Round the corner, past the flight of steps leading upwards into the darkness and along the last few yards. I felt the skin tighten in anticipation all over my body and in the same moment gave a low, involuntary cry. We had rounded the last corner into the short passage ending in the dirty-paned window. On our right was the door through which I had spoken to Etienne —and it stood open.

I heard Carl's muttered exclamation, then he reached past me and, caution forgotten, flicked on the light. We all stood blinking in the sudden brightness at the empty room before us. There was no window in this inside room. The old trolley was in its place just inside the door, a rickety chair beside it, and a rusty bedstead was propped against the far wall. There was no sign whatever of recent habitation, nothing at all that could give us any clue about the prisoner who had been held here so lately. I felt their doubt, caught their exchanged glances.

"You're sure this was the room, Ginnie?"

"Of course I'm sure. Rachel must have known I knew what those dishes were. They've moved him somewhere else and we're back to square one, with not a shred of evidence to prove he was ever here." My voice cracked with disappointment.

"Well, there's not much to be gained here," Marcus said briskly, "and I don't mind admitting this place gives me the creeps. If they've moved him he won't be in this building at all, that's clear, so let's get out and decide what to do next."

I felt incapable of further thought, bowed down by a sense of anticlimax. Silently we retraced our steps along the passages, down the stairs and out into the mews. Spiritlessly I dropped the key through Bert's lopsided letterbox and, still in dejected silence, we walked back to the car.

"Any ideas, Ginnie?" Carl asked at last. "You know them all better than we do. What are they most likely to have done with him?"

"I can't imagine," I said hopelessly. Having counted on the whole thing being settled tonight, I was still numb with disappointment.

"Come on now, think. Where might they have taken him?"

"I don't know, I tell you."

We were standing grouped round the car, shivering a little with the aftermath of excitement and the chilly evening air.

"You reckon only the Derbyshires and Laurence were in on it?"

"Yes, I'm almost sure."

"Could they have hidden him in one of their homes?"

"Not Laurence, anyway. Suzanne would—" I straight-ened suddenly as a ray of hope at last came to me. "She's much more likely to know what they'd do than I am."

"Then phone her. Now." Marcus led me briskly to the lighted call box on the opposite corner of the road. "Get her to come and meet us straightaway."

"At the flat?"

"The pub across the road there would be better, and she could get here quicker."

My fingers were stiff on the dial but at last the phone rang in my ear and a moment later Laurence's voice said clearly, "Westhampton 258."

I muffled the mouthpiece with my hand. "Laurence, it's Joanna. Could I have a word with Suzanne?"

"Just a minute, Jo."

And then Suzanne's voice, staccato and strained. "Joanna?"

I said rapidly, "Suzanne, it's Ginnie Clements. Don't say a thing—just listen. I must see you straightaway—it's about Etienne. Can you slip out on some pretext and meet me at the Bear and Garter in Wicklow Street?"

I could hear her rapid, accelerated breathing. You're an actress, girl! I exhorted her silently. Act now as you've never done before!

"I'll be there," she said at last, and the phone clicked. I pushed open the heavy door and rejoined Carl and Marcus. "She's coming."

"Good. Let's warm ourselves up with a drink while we're waiting."

The pub was small and old and covered with horse brasses. There was a wide brick fireplace with settles on either side and copper kettles gleaming on the hearth. I longed to sit by the hugely roaring fire, but realized this would be too public for Carl and Suzanne, both of whom were quite likely to be recognized. We chose the end booth against the wall and Marcus went to the bar to order drinks. We had been there only ten minutes when she came, fragile and lovely in a suede jacket with shaggy white fur at wrists and neck. She hesitated for a moment when she saw I was not alone, but I nodded encouragingly and she came over and slid into the booth next to Carl, leaving Marcus and myself to face any eyes that might be turned in our direction.

I introduced the two men to her swiftly, then leaned towards her across the table. "Listen, Suzanne, you were right about Etienne not going away willingly but wrong about it having nothing to do with anyone from the theatre. He's been there all the time, locked away in one of the unused storerooms under the stage."

She stared at me dumbly, her eyes enormous in her white face.

"Laurence knew, I'm afraid," I went on a little awkwardly, "and Stephen and Rachel. No one else, I think."

Her eyes swivelled to Carl beside her. "So it was something to do with Etienne, your coming down here before."

"Yes," he answered solemnly.

I could see the various thoughts chasing each other across her beautiful, expressive face, doubt, indignation, incredulity and then, suddenly, fear. "If you know where he is, why aren't you down there letting him out? What do you want with me?" Her voice rose. "Something else has happened, hasn't it? Something you haven't told me."

I put my hand quickly over hers. "On Friday afternoon I found Rachel washing up his lunch things in the kitchen. She pretended they were Stephen's and I pretended to believe her, but she and Stephen had been wondering for some time whether I knew more than I should and they must have decided they daren't take the risk. We've just been to the theatre, Suzanne, and he's gone."

"Gone?" She stared wildly from one of us to the other.

"That's why we need your help, to see if you can think of anywhere they could possibly have taken him."

Marcus pushed her glass slightly towards her. She took the hint and drank a few gulps of the fiery liquid.

"Laurence is in on it?" she repeated, the facts beginning to sink in. "He must have seen us together, he or Stephen." She looked up suddenly. "I think I know where they'll have taken him, then." The three of us waited breathlessly. "We have a cottage, Laurence and I, down on the coast, near Lymington. It's locked up all through the winter, no one ever goes near it, it's right out on the cliffs." Fear clamped like a mask over her face. "But they couldn't expect to look after him properly at that distance!" It was a thought that, I knew by the others' expressions, had occurred to us all simultaneously. "What are they going to do with him? Oh, God, they might have done something already!" Her long tapering fingers trembled against her mouth.

"There's no time to lose, certainly," Carl said bracingly. "Can you lead us straight to the place?"

"Yes, yes, of course. It's about a two-hour drive, though."

Carl murmured to me, "I must just phone Madame and put her in the picture. She'll be waiting for a call."

I said softly, "Try to minimize the danger."

Suzanne stood up to let him pass, then sank down again, her head in her hands, the sleek cap of black hair falling across her fingers. She said brokenly, "It'll be my fault if anything happens to him. All this happened because of me."

Marcus and I looked at each other helplessly and did not reply. A moment later Carl was back. "Right, off we go again." He took Suzanne's arm and led her out of the pub, Marcus and myself bringing up the rear. Suddenly Marcus said, "You go on with them. I won't be a moment."

The three of us crossed to the car and sat inside waiting and after a while Marcus appeared, a package in his hand. "It occurred to me that probably none of us has had anything to eat since lunch so I got some sandwiches. Unfortunately they hadn't any coffee."

"Good thinking," Carl said briefly. He waited while Marcus settled in the back seat beside Suzanne. "Now, which way do we go from here? I haven't a map of this area, I'm afraid."

"I can guide you as far as the coast," Marcus offered, "if Suzanne can take over once we get to Lymington. We want the Andover road first. Turn left at the bottom here and left again at the traffic lights and that brings you onto it."

"What excuse did you give Laurence for leaving the house?" I asked Suzanne.

"Nothing, really; he was upstairs. I just called that I was going out for a while to see Joanna."

"What time will he start expecting you back?"

"In about an hour or so, I imagine. He'll probably phone Jo eventually when I don't turn up."

"And when he hears she never contacted you—"

"He'll guess what's happening," Marcus cut in. "Is there a phone at the cottage?"

"Lord, no, we go there to get away from telephones."

"Then he'll have no way of warning whoever's down there that we might be on our way. In which case, he'll probably set out for Lymington himself."

Suzanne held her wrist up to the car window and peered at her watch. "We've still a bit of time in hand, I should think. We ought to have about half an hour's start on him, but he drives like the very devil."

"Then we must do the same." Carl's foot went down and the car leaped forward through the last remaining outskirts of Westhampton and out into the windswept darkness of the surrounding countryside.

Chapter 15

FOR the most part we travelled in silence. The noise of the car's rushing progress made conversation difficult and we were all wrapped up in our own thoughts, wondering what would be awaiting us at the lonely cottage on the cliff. At one stage Marcus handed round the sandwiches, moist and flavoursome ham, and though we ate mechanically I doubt if any of us was aware of hunger.

Once Carl said, almost under his breath, "Of course, Laurence might not have waited as long as an hour before phoning Joanna—" I knew his concern was far more for Madame, anxiously waiting in London, than for the prisoner himself.

"Those lights over there are Southampton," Marcus informed us as we came down into Cadham. "Now we've just got the New Forest to negotiate and we're there. Turn off here onto the A337."

The car swerved obediently under Carl's hands. I glanced at his face but it was set and grim, eyes intent on the road racing under our wheels. I thought pulsatingly, I hope it's

Rachel with him. I didn't fancy the thought of Stephen, cornered and at bay with the gun which might or might not be real.

"Right, Suzanne," Marcus said at last, "we're just approaching Lymington now. Can you take over from here?"

She leaned forward between Carl and myself, her breath sweet and warm on my cheek as she directed Carl down narrow twisting roads which gradually opened out onto a bare, deserted cliff road, degenerating beneath our wheels into a rough, rock-hewn track.

"Now!" she said suddenly, her voice vibrant with excitement. "There it is, over there."

"It's in darkness," Marcus said jerkily.

Nobody made any comment. Carl bumped to a halt outside a tiny gate gleaming white in the headlamps and we eased our cramped bodies out of the car and stood shivering as the stiff sea breeze slammed into us. Suzanne set off at a stumbling run up the short path to the front door, and her cry as she reached it was caught by the wind and tossed into the turbulent air like the call of some seabird. She turned back to face us as we hurried after her, her hair whipping stingingly across her face. "It's not locked! They must be here."

"Let me go first." Carl pushed her gently to one side and I perforce bit back my automatic protest. Then we were all crowding into the room which lay directly beyond and Suzanne's fingers were clawing madly at the light switch. For the second time that evening we stood blinking at an unexpectedly empty room. Only this one wasn't empty after all.

Carl said sharply, "Keep the girls back!" and moved

swiftly round the sofa, kneeling down to examine what lay behind.

"Etienne?" Suzanne demanded on a high note of hysteria, and he replied quickly, "No, I imagine it's Rachel, and I think she's still alive."

"Rachel? Then—" Suzanne's eyes went wildly round the blue painted walls and she darted towards the other doors, flinging them open and switching on light after light. Kitchen, bathroom and bedroom were all deserted. Once again there was no sign whatever of Etienne Lefevre. Marcus said suddenly, "Carl, someone's coming!"

We all turned instinctively as outside in the darkness headlights blossomed, another car skidded to a halt and two figures came running up the path. A moment later Laurence and Stephen Darby stood staring at us from the doorway.

Carl said crisply, "There's no time for histrionics. Darby, your sister's hurt. It looks as though she's been lying here for some hours."

"Lefevre?" Laurence rapped out as Stephen hurried to join Carl. Marcus shrugged eloquently. Laurence's eyes went to his wife's white, accusing face. He half put out a hand towards her but she shrank away and he hopelessly let it drop and moved instead to join the two men kneeling on the floor. "How bad is it?"

"Bad enough," Carl said tensely. "We oughtn't to move her really but it would be quicker to take her to the nearest hospital than have to rush off to find a phone and then wait for an ambulance to find its way here. Do you agree?" His eyes briefly raked Stephen's white, drawn face. Stephen nodded and moistened his lips.

"Do you think she has a chance?"

"It depends what her injuries are. There's a nasty wound in her head here, but it's so caked and matted with blood and hair that I can't see how bad it is." He looked up, undisputedly in command of us and the situation—as always, I thought resignedly. "We'll say," he went on deliberately, "that she was alone in the cottage and must have been attacked by an intruder. Stephen came down because she'd been expected back in Westhampton this afternoon and he was anxious. The rest of us don't have to come into it at all."

"What about you?" Laurence said hoarsely. "Whoever goes to the hospital will have to make a statement to the police. It would be better if I went with Steve; after all, it would be natural for me to have come with him. You're too well-known to avoid national publicity."

"Then the three of us will go and I'll stay in the car."

Laurence smiled mirthlessly. "You mean you don't trust us to come back here."

"No," Carl answered calmly, "and we have quite a lot of talking to do." His eyes moved to the rest of us. "Marcus, will you stay here with the girls? We shouldn't be long. There might be some food or drink?" He looked enquiringly at Laurence, but it was Stephen who answered numbly.

"Rachel brought some provisions down yesterday." His voice cracked and he put his hand across his eyes.

"Come on then," Carl instructed, a little more gently, "help me to lift her as carefully as possible."

Suzanne and I stood helplessly while the four men manoeuvred the limp body out of the room, down the path and into the back seat of Laurence's car. Moments later Marcus came back and shut the door.

"There's an electric fire over there, Ginnie. Switch it on,

207

will you? And, Suzanne, you know where everything's kept. Do you think you could manage some coffee? I'm sure we could all do with it."

I said shakily, "Do you think Carl will be all right with them? Suppose they don't agree to come back?"

"Knowing we're here and know everything? Of course they'll come. Don't worry, love." He gave my hand a little pat.

"But where can Etienne be?" Suzanne asked tremulously. "I can't bear to think of him on the run again, hungry and hiding like he was before."

"How about that coffee?" Marcus reminded her. "Come on, we'll all get it together. The others will need it when they get back."

It was almost an hour before in fact the three of them returned.

"What's the news?" I asked quickly, looking fearfully at their white, strained faces.

"She's having an emergency operation now. We're to ring the hospital in an hour." It was Carl who had answered. Marcus nodded to me to produce the coffee, but my hand was shaking so much that a lot of it went into the saucers.

"We came down here yesterday morning," Stephen began jerkily, as though knowing the time for explanations could no longer be delayed. "Rachel was sure Ginnie suspected about Lefevre. This was just to be a temporary hideout till we had time to work out what to do. I had to go straight back to be in time for the matinee. I'm not in the next production and I was going to come back to join her tomorrow. What with the party last night I didn't feel like making the journey today. I wish to God I had, though." His voice shook. "They said at the hospital she'd been unconscious for over twenty-four hours. He must have attacked her and got away almost as soon as I left. God, I thought we'd made it once we got here; the journey was a nightmare. I kept thinking he'd try to attract attention or something, but the gun must have done the trick."

Suzanne said ringingly, "How could you do it, both of you? What on earth possessed you to kidnap him in the first place?"

Laurence said heavily, "The short answer to that is jealousy. That and greed, and the desire for revenge. It's hard to credit it, looking back, but it was all done on the spur of the moment. We regretted it almost immediately but it was already too late."

"How did you find out?" Suzanne asked in a whisper.

"I happened to be driving back along the Amesbury road and saw you both go into the Picardy. You must admit that was pretty conclusive."

"And you told Stephen?" she demanded incredulously.

"In a manner of speaking. In point of fact I went straight home and got very drunk. Stephen came round to see why I didn't show up at the theatre for a meeting that afternoon. I was pretty far gone by then and blurted the whole thing out. At the time he just concentrated on sobering me up in time for the performance, but he came to my dressing room after it was over."

Stephen eyed us belligerently. "All right, I admit I was the chief instigator. I just didn't see why Lefevre should get away with it."

209

"Go on," said Carl coldly.

"Well, the theatre was in dire financial straits as usual and when Etienne had been with us he'd never stopped going on about all the money his mother had. To be fair, he brought quite a sheaf of it down once, to repay us for—" He broke off, plainly wondering how much we knew.

"For smuggling him into the country," Carl finished for him.

Stephen flushed uncomfortably. "Yes. Well, anyway, we knew he'd no money of his own—that was obvious—and we also knew his mother would be unlikely to pay for the privilege of his being with Suzanne. But we did think she'd be prepared to fork out if his actual life seemed to be in danger, and what's more, under the circumstances she wouldn't have dared to go to the police. It seemed foolproof. We thought it would all be over in a couple of days. In the meantime we could hide him out in the theatre and Rachel could be called on to provide food. Best of all, we knew that even when we let him go, he couldn't report us for obvious reasons."

"What we hadn't reckoned on," Laurence put in heavily, "was that she wouldn't believe our note was genuine. At least, we imagined it must be that because she ignored it completely. Then we really were in a mess."

"One of you went to the Picardy to collect him?" Marcus prompted.

"Yes. We knew that Suzanne would make enquiries there, so it had to look as though he'd left voluntarily. The next morning Laurence kept her out of the way—"

"Of course!" Suzanne broke in. "That new outfit you suddenly insisted I needed for the third act!"

210

"—and I went to the hotel and told him Suzanne wanted to see him urgently at the theatre. He went with me like a lamb, but things started to go wrong straightaway. There was that foul-up of the phone call." His eyes moved to my face. "It *was* you who took it, wasn't it?" I nodded. "And of course Rachel's accident meant I had to see to him all the time. On top of that, the note brought forth nothing whatever and to cap it all Ginnie here kept turning up with her big, innocent eyes and guileless questions."

"So you tried to frighten me off," I said steadily.

"Yes, phone calls and Sam and Teddy in the park. But you didn't frighten easily, did you?" He glanced at Marcus. "I presume it was you I tangled with on the balcony? Sorry about the left hook."

"What were you doing there, anyway?"

"I was only going to force the window open. I wouldn't have touched her." He turned to Carl. "I hope you believe that."

"Go on," Carl instructed grimly.

"I imagine you know all the rest." He looked at our faces in frightened defiance. "Well, what are you going to do about it? Nothing that I've told you can be proved in any way and naturally Laurence and I will deny everything."

"What I don't understand," Marcus said, leaning forward to put his coffee cup down, "is why, since the ransom note obviously wasn't going to work, you didn't simply give up and let him go."

"It's easy to be logical now," Laurence said bitterly. "Of course that's what we should have done, and actually what we were finally going to do, tomorrow, in sheer desperation."

211

"But why hang on so long? In case his mother finally gave way after all?"

"Partly that; we felt time might be on our side and the strain would eventually begin to tell. And also"—Laurence's eyes flicked to his wife and away again—"releasing him would mean he was free to go back to Suzanne. He'd tell her the whole story and she would probably have gone off with him and become as much a fugitive as he was. I couldn't risk that until I'd no alternative." Suzanne's eyes had filled with tears. Ignoring the rest of us, he turned to her. "Darling, I'm sorry, I know these last few weeks have been hell for you, but believe me they have for me too. Let him go. It would be an impossible life for you, always only one jump ahead of the police."

We all waited motionless for her reply but she merely shook her head and covered her face with her hands. Obviously the spell of Etienne Lefevre was not broken yet.

Stephen's voice was loud in the stillness, making me jump. "It's almost time to ring the hospital. Where's the nearest phone, Laurence?"

Laurence wrenched his eyes away from Suzanne's bent head. "At the bottom of the hill. I'll come with you."

This time no one suggested that they might not return. It didn't seem to matter, anyway. The rest of us waited in almost total silence and in fifteen minutes they were back.

"The operation was a success, apparently, but they won't really be able to gauge her chances for another few hours yet." Stephen wiped his hand across his face. "I'll stay down here, of course, but there's nothing to keep the rest of you. Laurence left his name in case the police want to contact him. Is there anything else the police have to know?" His pathetic attempt at a challenge made me wonder how I had ever been frightened of him. Carl shook his head for the rest of us. "Right, then you might as well be going. I'm sorry to have caused all this trouble. If it's any comfort, I'm paying for it now."

Nobody replied. Laurence went over and put his hand gently on Suzanne's shoulder. She looked up, her face dazed. "He might come back here. Perhaps I should stay—"

"This is the last place he'll come," Stephen said shortly. "For all he knows, he could have killed Rachel. It's my bet he's miles away by now, probably on the way back to Mama."

I met Carl's startled glance. "God, I never thought of that. We'd better stop at that phone box ourselves and warn her. He could have arrived there hours ago."

Laurence helped Suzanne to her feet and she allowed him to lead her to the door. Stephen's eyes, brooding and unreadable, followed them. At the door Laurence turned and addressed Carl. "It may sound trite, but would you pass on my very sincere apologies to Madame Lefevre and thank her for not taking things any further. I can promise you we've all learned our lesson. I just hope to God Rachel—" He bit his lip, glanced at Stephen and away again and, his arm still round Suzanne, went out of the house.

Marcus said quietly, "If you don't mind, I'll stay with Stephen. I don't think he should be alone. I'll phone you in the morning with any news."

Stephen said with difficulty, "There's no need—"

"I'd like to."

"Then thank you." He turned away abruptly, the unexpected act of kindness too much for his already shaken control.

Carl stood up. "Ready then, Ginnie?"

Marcus said to me, "If I don't see you again—"

"You will," I interrupted quickly. "I'll be in Westhampton at least till the end of the week. Good night, Marcus, and thank you."

He nodded and I went with Carl out into the strong sea wind. It was just after ten-thirty. At this time yesterday I had been sitting outside the London flat waiting for Carl's return. A traumatic twenty-four hours. We stopped at the call box at the bottom of the hill and Carl phoned Madame. "She hasn't heard a thing," he told me as he came back to the car. "Poor soul, she doesn't know what to think now, and of course she's extremely concerned about Rachel, though I didn't tell her how badly hurt she is."

"Do you think she'll live?" I asked fearfully.

"I suppose it depends on the brain damage. She could be in a coma for weeks; you hear of such things."

I must have slept on the way home, for I remember little of the journey. Fortunately even without Suzanne and Marcus to guide him, Carl managed to find the right road and it was just after midnight when we arrived back at the Beeches. I directed him round to the garage and we walked back with the help of the torch he had taken to the theatre hours before. The days of fear, of looking back over my shoulder, were finished. Never again should I have to walk home through the dark alone.

It was as we sat in the minute, sun-filled kitchen over breakfast the next morning that the final piece of the jigsaw fell neatly into place. The current affairs program on the radio had been providing a background to our desultory conversation and it was pure chance that the vital words happened to fall into a pause in our talking.

"Southampton police say that a man is helping with their enquiries into the holdup of an off-license in the area on Saturday evening, in which the manager was knocked unconscious. They are examining the possibility of a link between this attack and that on a woman in a remote cottage outside Lymington the same evening. The woman, Miss Rachel Derbyshire, aged twenty-six, was discovered by her brother last night and rushed to hospital where she underwent an emergency operation. Police have named the man as Etienne Lefevre, a Frenchman who escaped from St. Luc prison last July. It is not yet known how he managed to enter this country, as he insists he has neither friends nor relatives here. The French police have applied for an extradition order. If anyone has any information which might shed a light on Lefevre's movements during the last three months, the number to ring is—"

Carl reached over and switched off the set. "Well, well," he said softly, "all in all, it's the best thing that could happen, certainly for Laurence and Madame anyway."

"If Rachel dies, he'll be on a murder charge," I reminded him. The phone shrilled in the hall. "That'll be Marcus now." There was a hard lump of apprehension in my chest.

"I'll go." Carl went through and I could hear him relaying the news we had just heard. Slowly I pushed back my chair and went to the doorway, leaning against the frame and staring down at the green carpet.

Carl replaced the phone. "All right, honey, you can go to

work now with an easy mind. Rachel has regained consciousness and it looks as though she's going to pull through. I'll drive you to the George and then come back and phone Madame and the Greys."

On the familiar journey through the streets of Westhampton, my mind revolved round the happenings of the last weeks, the people I had met and the situations that had arisen. If I hadn't found Carl with Leonie, would the fate of Etienne, Rachel, Suzanne, have been any different? It was impossible to unravel all the threads, to pick out one which could have altered the pattern of the events that followed.

"Here we are." Carl pulled up outside the hotel and leaned across to kiss me. "Don't worry any more, sweetheart. Everything will be all right now. I'll come back and join you for lunch."

I nodded and watched him drive away with a wave of his hand. Then I turned and walked slowly up the steps of the George, which, I reflected with a slight smile, just about brought me round full circle.

DATE DUE

OCT 2 6 1976	FEB 5 1979		
DEC 1 5 1976	MAR 1 2 1979		
APR 1 2 1977	OCT 1 1979		
AUG 1 1 1977			
NOV 1 1 1977	NOV 6 1979		
JAN 1 6 1978	JAN 2 8 1980		
JAN 3 '78	DE 8 '83		
	JA 31 '84		
JAN 18 '78	MR 12 '84		
FEB 6 '78	AP 30 '84		
FEB 13 '78	JY 2 '84		
MAR 1 4 1978	NO 27 '84		
MAY 8 '78			
MAY 2 '78	JAN 2 1 1985		
NOV 3 0 1978	MAR 1 6 1990		
JAN 8 '79			
DEC. 1 9 1978			
JAN 3 1979			
E. AKIN			
GAYLORD			PRINTED IN U.S.A